KU-024-828

This one is for Imogen Taylor, with huge thanks

DEBORAH MOGGACH

THE CARER

TINDER
PRESS

Copyright © 2019 Deborah Moggach

The right of Deborah Moggach to be identified as the Author of
the Work has been asserted by her in accordance with the
Copyright, Designs and Patents Act 1988.

First published in Great Britain in 2019 by Tinder Press
An imprint of HEADLINE PUBLISHING GROUP

2

Apart from any use permitted under UK copyright law, this publication
may only be reproduced, stored, or transmitted, in any form, or by any
means, with prior permission in writing of the publishers or, in the case
of reprographic production, in accordance with the terms of licences
issued by the Copyright Licensing Agency.

All characters in this publication are fictitious and any resemblance to real
persons, living or dead, is purely coincidental.

Cataloguing in Publication Data is available from the British Library

Hardback ISBN 978 1 4722 6048 2
Trade paperback ISBN 978 1 4722 6046 8

Typeset in Sabon LT Std 10.75/14.5 pt by Jouve (UK), Milton Keynes

Printed and bound in Great Britain by Clays Ltd, Elcograf S.p.A.

MIX
Paper from
responsible sources
FSC® C104740

Headline's policy is to use papers that are natural, renewable and recyclable
products and made from wood grown in well-managed forests and other
controlled sources. The logging and manufacturing processes are expected
to conform to the environmental regulations of the country of origin.

HEADLINE PUBLISHING GROUP
An Hachette UK Company
Carmelite House
50 Victoria Embankment
London EC4Y 0DZ

www.tinderpress.co.uk
www.headline.co.uk
www.hachette.co.uk

CAVAN COUNTY LIBRARY
ACC No. S/16931
CLASS NO. F
INVOICE NO. 11370 ILS
PRICE €11.01

PART ONE

Phoebe

The first thing she noticed was her skin. So smooth, for somebody of fifty. Eerily smooth, but then Mandy had never had children – never been married, as far as Phoebe knew – none of the normal wear and tear that makes a woman look used.

Mandy was not beautiful – far from it. An overweight woman with Rosemary West specs, wearing a bobble hat and stripy tights, something vaguely blokey about her. Some time later she told Phoebe: 'I tried to be a lesbian once but it just didn't gel. Give me a man any day. I like the smell of their armpits.'

Phoebe liked her, truly she did. She'd come to the rescue after her father had his fall. Two carers had come and gone. Rejoice, from Zimbabwe, who talked all through his beloved Radio 4 and fed him some sort of maize-meal that clogged up his bowels. Then there was Teresa from County Donegal, who was having a love affair with a baggage-handler from Luton Airport and who sat texting him, in a fug of cigarette smoke, and reading out the replies while the kettle boiled dry and Dad dehydrated.

So Mandy came to the rescue: Mandy from Solihull, arriving in her trusty Fiat Panda and bearing home-made shortbread because her speciality, flapjacks, played havoc with an old boy's dentures. Phoebe, normally wary, was

3

encouraged by this early sign of empathy. Mandy hummed show tunes as the kettle boiled. *Blood Brothers* was her favourite, about two boys separated at birth. She said she had seen it three times and blubbed like a baby.

Phoebe understood why, later. At the time she was simply grateful that this bulky, chatty woman had entered their lives and restored her sanity. Her father's, too. For within days Mandy had become essential.

It was a wild autumn in the village where her father lived. Branches were torn from trees and his lawn was strewn with twigs. The yapping dog next door was silenced by a seizure and was discovered a week later, stiff under a pile of leaves that had drifted against the wall. He was a Jack Russell and therefore a perpetual irritant, but the loss of his old enemy dimmed the gleam in her father's eye and plunged him further into gloom.

> *That time of year thou mayst in me behold*, he intoned,
> *When yellow leaves, or none, or few, do hang*
> *Upon those boughs which shake against the cold,*
> *Bare ruin'd choirs, where late the sweet birds sang.*

God knew why her parents had retired to the Cotswolds. The village was dead, utterly dead. Ghosts only lingered in the names: The Old Smithy, The Bakehouse ... honey-stone cottages whose inhabitants had long since gone. It woke up at weekends when the Londoners arrived in their Porsche Cayennes, stuffed with mutinous teenagers and Waitrose bags, and sank back into torpor when they left. What did her father *do* all day, in his diminished life? When her mother was alive he could bicker with her, as men do

who are dependent on their beloveds. Nowadays his main irritation was to shout at the coach drivers parked outside who, long after they had disgorged their Japanese tourists to wander round the village taking selfies, kept their bloody engines running, filling his living room with exhaust fumes.

Breaking his hip had shunted him into helplessness. No longer could he manage the stairs so a single bed was moved to the ground floor. Upstairs had been his marriage. For sixty-four years, at home and abroad, he had slumbered in mammalian warmth, his wife beside him, deep in her unknowable dreams. Now he slept downstairs like a wizened teenager, alone in his chaste bed, returned full circle to his youth. The room faced the street. One morning he opened his curtains to reveal a tourist at his window, gazing at her reflection as she applied her lipstick. 'I'm living in a blithering museum,' he grumbled. 'I'm a blithering waxwork.'

He wasn't by nature a morose man, he just missed his wife and hated getting old – who wouldn't? Most of his friends had died and by now there was nobody around who remembered the war. Even the ancients in the village turned out to be in their sixties, their faces prematurely aged by the blistering winds that blew across the bleak and lovely uplands.

No wonder his carers didn't stay long. Visitors shuffled round the Norman church and ate scones in the teashop, but there was nothing else to do and only one bus a day into the relatively throbbing town of Cirencester.

But Mandy didn't mind. Mandy didn't mind anything. There was something bracingly impervious about her – a necessity, Phoebe guessed, in her profession. She talked fondly about her previous patients and told Phoebe in detail about their debilitating ailments, the morphine drips and nappies and dementia.

'Dear Mrs Klein, she thought she was in a hotel but you have to just go with the flow, you know? She'd say, *I don't like this hotel*, so I'd pack her suitcase and walk her round the block. We'd arrive back at her house and I'd say, *This looks like a nicer hotel, doesn't it, dear? Oh yes*, she'd say, *I like this one better*. So we went in and unpacked her bag and she was as happy as Larry until she started fretting, so we'd do the whole thing all over again.' Mandy took a gulp from her thermal mug. 'I was holding her hand when she passed away, four in the morning. It's always four when they're called. The cat knew and so did I.' There was a strange exuberance in her voice when she told Phoebe this. 'She knew I'd be there for her.'

She arrived with testimonials from grateful families. They were lavish in their praise. Mandy's attitude to them, however, was dismissive.

'Catch *them* wiping their bums. No way, Jose! *They'd* had their bums wiped when they were babies, hadn't they? Didn't that come into their calculations? What goes round comes round. You reap what you sow. I think I was a Hindu in another life.'

These conversations made Phoebe uncomfortable, but who was she to complain? Mandy had come to her rescue.

And how swiftly she made herself at home! Within a week it felt she had been there for ever. When the door was ajar Phoebe glanced into Mandy's bedroom and was startled by the transformation. A crochet coverlet, sewn with blowsy flowers, lay tangled on the bed. On it slumped a fluffy dachshund, a nightie poking from its zippered belly. She had removed a painting on the wall and replaced it with a pegboard, filled with snapshots of herself and various girlfriends in holiday locations. Not a man in sight. On the chest of drawers were crammed an assortment of knick-knacks – china animals, that sort of thing – and a framed photograph of her parents on their wedding day. Clothes were strewn everywhere; it was her inner sanctum and Phoebe blushed at the intrusion.

She didn't feel uneasy, not then. She was just pleased at this sign of permanent occupation. For, by God, she needed Mandy. So did her brother, Robert.

Robert lived in Wimbledon and she lived in Wales. Their father's village lay between the two of them. In recent years, as various crises had arisen, there had been some tense exchanges between them about who should make the journey. Robert was nearer, but traffic was diabolical, getting out of London. He also subtly reminded Phoebe that he was a family man, with commitments. In fact his children had long since left home and all he did was sit in his garden shed trying to write but she didn't like to point this out, because mentioning his novel wasn't advisable, dear me no.

Phoebe, however, was a single woman, of a certain age, and childless. This suggested an Austen-like obligation to devote herself to others, but she was buggered if she'd let Robert off the hook. Theirs was a turbulent relationship. In adult life it had been flimsily cling-filmed with good manners but skirmishes could still erupt, especially when alcohol was involved.

Mandy, however, eased all this. 'Don't you worry about a

thing.' She stood in the doorway, her glasses flashing in the sunlight. 'I'm here now, and everything'll be tickety-boo.' Phoebe gazed at that smooth face, unweathered by the past. The woman was fifty! Did living for others keep one young?

She knew little about Mandy, in those early days. All she knew was that she'd arrived with her orange teapot and Marigold gloves, their saviour from Solihull, to take over their father's life and release them back to theirs.

Phoebe was busy setting up her exhibition of watercolours. It was in the waiting room of her local doctors' surgery but she hoped that this might be to its advantage. After all, people facing a smear test might be comforted by one of her sheep. They might even, God forbid, buy one. She'd also put up a display of her latest works on glass – drinking tumblers painted with wild flowers. She'd actually sold a couple of these at the recent Craft Fayre at the British Legion. Both were of cow parsley, so she'd been concentrating on the *umbelliferae* family for this display – sweet cicely, chervil, that sort of thing.

All artists struggle, of course. She wasn't ready to cut off her ear but she was becoming increasingly dispirited. Trouble was, in her small Welsh town the market was saturated. Every second person was an artist, most of them women. Hares and sheep, sheep and hares, that's what they painted and they were all at it. The results of their labours were displayed along the High Street – in the newsagent's window, hanging on the walls of The Coffee Cup, even propped on easels amongst the bedroom slippers, saucepans and dusty, nightie-clad mannequin that leaned drunkenly in the window of Audrey's Emporium, a shop hilariously unchanged for as long as anyone could remember.

Much remained unchanged in Knockton. Unlike her father's village, however, it wasn't dead; it was a thriving little town with plenty of independent shops. Phoebe lived up the alley behind the butcher's, in what had been the abattoir. Her studio overlooked the back yard and she worked to the percussive thump of the meat cleaver as it dismembered the very animals she was attempting to depict.

She couldn't have a private view, not in a doctors' surgery. However, she was curious to see how people reacted to her artworks so she dropped in, on the pretext of getting a repeat prescription for the oestrogen pessaries that should be making sex with Torren less excruciating. Three people sat in the waiting room, all of them busy on their phones. The display cabinet, in which she'd put her tumblers, was now covered with a blue sateen sheet upon which was arranged a Nutribite promotion, complete with smoothie goblet and a bowl of plastic fruit.

At that moment her own phone rang. It was Mandy. 'How are you today?' she asked. 'Just checking in. We've had a lovely morning, haven't we, Jimmy?'

Jimmy? Nobody called her father Jimmy. His name was James.

'I gave him a foot massage, he was purring like a pussy-cat, weren't you, love? He says he's never had one before but it certainly put a smile on his face and his blood pressure's way down. It'll also help with his constipation. Then we wrapped up warmly and went down the lane to say hello to the donkeys. Next time we'll bring them some sugar-lumps, won't we, pet? I have to say it's a real pleasure, looking after your dad. He's such a gentleman, and so interesting. He's been telling me all about his work at the university. Would you like to say hello to your daughter?'

Her father came on the line. He sounded in fine spirits, but he was always so polite it was hard to tell what he was really thinking.

'Mandy's been entertaining me with stories about her previous old crocks. Most amusing,' he said. 'One of them was a devout Catholic and she took him to Lourdes in the hope of a miracle. While he was away being blessed or whatever, Mandy sat down in a wheelchair and had a snooze.' He started chuckling. 'And when she woke up – when she woke up . . .' He stopped, wheezing with laughter. 'You tell her, Mandy.'

'So I woke up and walked off—'

'– she *rose* from her wheelchair,' Dad said, his voice shaking. 'And when she did that, everyone stared at her and dropped to their knees—'

'And started praying!' Mandy grabbed back the phone. 'See, they thought it was a miracle. Get it?'

'Yes, I got it,' Phoebe said.

Her father, still snuffling with laughter, took back the phone. 'From now on I'm calling her Saint Mandy, Patron Saint of Lost Specs.'

Phoebe laughed too, of course. Her father sounded more cheerful than he had been for ages.

'She's a tonic, this girl,' he said.

'*Girl?*' She could hear Mandy snorting with laughter.

'At my age, you're all girls,' he said. 'Youth is wasted on the young.'

Mandy gave a squeal. 'That's a funny thing to say.'

'It's Mr Shaw who said it.'

'Who's he?' she asked. 'Another of your intellectual friends?' She grabbed the phone. 'Your father has been trying to explain to me what he actually does – *did* – but I'm a simple sausage.'

'Particle physics,' Phoebe said. 'Me neither.'

Standing there in the doctors' surgery she felt that familiar sinking sensation. All her life she'd felt inadequate. It was one of the few things she had in common with her brother.

For their father was a serious intellectual – professorships, books, groundbreaking research. Robert had spent his life trying to compete, but she had taken another path. Both of them had been waving for his attention. It was the one thing, however, that he seemed incapable of giving them.

Even in the cottage. Even in Wales.

Robert

Robert was sitting in his shed, allegedly writing his novel. In fact he was thinking about his mother's death, and his sister's subtle upstaging in the grief stakes. Phoebe had always done this sort of thing, making him feel just that little bit less sensitive than she was herself. He remembered it so well, the three of them sitting around Mum, lifeless in her hospital bed. That waxen face, so familiar and yet not hers at all, an empty mother with her mouth open in a final, prehistoric yawn.

Phoebe turned to their father. 'Would you like to be alone with her for a while?'

Of course. Why hadn't he thought of that? Point one to Phoebe.

And then, when he'd gone in to say goodbye to what can only be described as a corpse, it was Phoebe's turn. She spent ages in there, much longer than he, and emerged with her face streaming with tears. She hugged their father, as if only the two of them truly understood the depth of their grief, and carried on crying all the way home, even fishing in Robert's pocket for his unused little pack of Kleenex. Point two to her.

He hadn't cried at all. It just seemed a tremendous relief that their mother's suffering had finally ended. He did cry later but nobody witnessed this, not even his wife.

Point three: a bunch of wild flowers for the coffin, lovingly gathered from the local hedgerows. His lavish bouquet looked vulgar and corporate next to Phoebe's wilting tribute, a goodbye from the heart.

He'd noticed this with terminal cancer. It creates a subtle sense of rivalry between the relatives – who saw the patient the most frequently, who brought the most thoughtful food, who had been given the most information about their medication, who became the favoured visitor who had a long, intimate and revelatory conversation with the loved one just before they passed away, who grieved the most copiously. And then there were the acquaintances who appeared from nowhere and muscled in – people who're good at death, people who're suddenly in their element. Like it or not, they become bustlingly indispensable and then fade back into obscurity. Mostly women, of course.

Bloody complicated, women. His mother, his sister, his wife. He was sixty-two and still hadn't got the hang of them. It was like those circuit boxes in the street. Plain boxes, so boring you hardly notice them. That's men. Then somebody from British Telecom opens them up and you're astonished by the thousands of tiny wires all tangled up but with their own baffling logic. That's them. Women.

His mother, for instance. She'd been just as brainy as his dad. They met at Oxford where she got a First in PPE. Photographs of the time showed a serious, high-minded student. Even in those yellowing snapshots she looked intimidating, her hair cropped in a bob around her striking face with its sharp cheekbones. A woman incapable of compromise.

But that's exactly what she did. Because first he and then

Phoebe were born, and bang went her hopes of a career in the civil service. She could have been a high-flyer; she could have been a Dame. In fact, she would have made a marvellous Prime Minister – principled and humourless and scrupulously fair. Instead she became a stuck-at-home mum. She wasn't so great at that.

In those days, women did the child-rearing, whatever simmering resentments they might have felt. And while she changed their nappies, their father was becoming more and more successful, whizzing off to conferences, hobnobbing with the great and good, gathering honours and generally charming everyone he met. For he was a charmer – attractive and funny and self-deprecating. His colleagues loved him, his students loved him, everybody loved him.

His carer loved him, and she'd only been there a month. 'He's such a dear,' Mandy said. '*Such* a gent, with that twinkle in his eye. We've been having a hoot!'

A hoot!

Robert looked at his watch. One o'clock; the morning had flown by. A dead wasp lay on his laptop. They seemed to hibernate in the shed, then conk out in the fumes from the paraffin heater. After lunch, he conked out too. There was a sagging couch for his siesta, rammed against the wall.

Farida, his wife, laughed at his shed. 'We're living in a five-bedroomed house in one of the most sought-after streets in Wimbledon,' she said. 'You've got your own study, central heating, Eames chair, lovely view, sensor lighting. You've got the whole fucking house, which took us three years of building hell to make into our dream home, and every morning you solemnly traipse down the garden to sit in a nasty little hut where you're poisoned with fumes and showered with dead insects.'

Farida didn't understand the creative process. How only in his hut did Robert feel free. A novelist needs that sense of separation, of liberation. As he trudged across the lawn he could feel his normal life lifting off him and his characters crowding in. They waited to welcome him as he wedged shut the warped door and settled down in his sanctum.

As for his afternoon nap – who was to blame for that? The problem was that he never got a good night's sleep. Farida had to get up at four in the morning, to go to work at the TV studios. She had her clothes laid out, she tried to be quiet, but of course he woke. He heard the rustle as she pulled on her designer outfits, grunting with irritation when the zip stuck. Through the bathroom door came the faint hiss of the shower. Out of consideration for him she used to tiptoe out of the bedroom, carrying her high heels, but recently she seemed to have forgotten about this, and, if he *had* still been asleep, he was jolted awake by the tap-tapping across the floorboards and down the stairs. Was this new lack of consideration a sign of something more worrying? As their neighbour, Linda, said: 'I realised my marriage was over when I didn't leave him the last strawberry.'

Farida read the news on breakfast TV. Every morning Robert watched terrorism, torture and mass shootings stream through those glossy crimson lips. Sometimes, if they'd been quarrelling, he felt she was singling him out; a Damascus car bomb was all his fault. This was paranoid, of course, but that didn't stop him. And then her face would soften as she talked about a Royal baby, and all was forgiven.

He should have got used to it by now. She'd been doing the job for years but the strangeness of it could still hit him. He knew that face so intimately, but then so did millions of others. For two hours each morning he shared her with the nation. She was still stunningly beautiful – polished bronze skin, shiny blue-black hair. Of course men fantasised about her. *He* fantasised about her, when she was at one remove like this and subtly altered by being on screen. There was an undeniable erotic jolt in knowing that she belonged to everybody but it was only he who would hold her naked in his arms that night.

Though, to be frank, there hadn't been much activity in *that* department for some time. This was only to be expected, of course, in a long marriage. Theirs, however, went through a sea change when he lost his job in the City.

At first Farida was sympathetic. She was on *BBC London News* at the time and reported on the sorry exodus of the chaps who had been given the push. There she was in her Nicole Farhi suit, talking to camera, whilst behind her Robert himself could be glimpsed amongst the stream of men leaving Canary Wharf, transformed into shirt-sleeved hobos as they clutched their pitiful cardboard boxes.

Oh, she was fine at first. As time passed, however, something altered between them. Farida was hardly a natural nurse and Robert was a broken man. Broken, humiliated, lost, needy . . . all the things with which she had no patience. She liked a sparring partner; it was one of the things that had attracted him in the first place – her bright steeliness, her lack of sentimentality. On their second date, when he leaned across a candle-lit table and stroked her hand, she'd said: 'I don't do dote.'

She didn't do dote, she didn't do failure. In a way he respected this, whilst also wallowing in self-pity and resentment. Not a pretty sight, especially when slumming about in tracksuit bottoms all day and loading the dishwasher wrong.

During that period Robert thought a lot about his wheeler-dealing career, to which he was so spectacularly unsuited. He chose it to impress his wife and to be a man. But he also did it to impress his father. Look, I can be successful too! Underneath it all, he simply wanted to get his attention.

The story of his life.

After his nap he brooded on Mandy's words. It was a long time since he and his dad had had anything resembling a hoot. His visits had been based on filial duty and a desire to get the hell out of it before the rush-hour traffic built up on the A40. His father was now an enfeebled old man, mostly confined to an armchair. Robert's need to prove himself had all but disappeared. For a sea change had taken place in their relationship.

Robert got up from the couch and bundled away the blanket. It still smelled of his dog, after all these months, and was threaded with his beloved grey hairs. Unlike his wife, dogs *did* do dote, that was their point. Christ, he missed him.

Leaving his hut, Robert padded across to the kitchen in search of a digestive biscuit. As he rummaged in the larder he thought about his father and how things between them had changed after his mother's death. Until then, his parents had seemed indestructible. Their strong marriage had cemented them together in the bond that had brought him into the world and been the core of his life.

Since then his father's universe had shrunk. That was not surprising: his health had worsened; he was suddenly alone. And now he was flailing around for some sort of contact, like a sea anemone waving its tentacles. No doubt he was searching for his wife, and the reassuring solidity of the big life they had once led and that she had so tirelessly made possible. But it had all disappeared, leaving nothing but memories, and he had rapidly become helpless. Robert's complex feelings for him had simplified into something as crude as pity. This filled him with desolation. No wonder his jokes had dried up.

Mandy, however, had reinvigorated the old man. Thank God for Mandy! She phoned most days to tell Robert their news. Her voice cheered him; that Brummie accent hadn't started to grate. This chatty woman in her chunky, implausible outfits had been their salvation.

Phoebe

Mandy bought the old man a special clock for his birthday. Each hour depicted a different British bird, which burst into song when it struck.

'I bought it from the RSPB,' she said. 'They've really pushed the boat out with their merchandise, haven't they, Pops?'

Pops? Robert and Phoebe froze in their seats. Jack, Robert's son, stifled a giggle.

Their father, however, was delighted. 'Two minutes to four,' he said. 'Sssh, everybody!'

They sat there in silence. Jack's hand inched towards his mobile but Farida gave him a nudge. This was rich, Phoebe thought, considering Farida had spent the last half-hour on the phone herself, pacing the garden and aerating the lawn with her Louboutin ankle-boots.

Robert stared at the carpet, his lower lip stuck out. Phoebe knew that expression so well; when he was a boy he could nurse a grievance for weeks. Maybe he and Farida had had a row; all these years and he still hadn't learned that sulking got him nowhere in the face of her breezy indifference.

Their father raised a finger – *wait for it* – his eyes sparkling. Was he humouring Mandy or truly excited? And how did he feel about being called Pops? For God's sake, the man had an OBE.

The silence was broken by a chirrup from the kitchen. 'The garden warbler!' announced Dad, striking his knee in triumph. 'A shy little chap, saw one in the fig tree only last summer. As light as thistledown, and now he'll be sunning himself in Africa.' He turned to Jack and Alice. 'My darlings, be mindful of just one thing as you journey through this baffling and beautiful thing called life. Nothing that science can achieve will ever even begin to *begin* to approach the miracle of bird migration.'

Alice took his hand. How wonderfully simple was her love for her grandfather! Jack was the same. They were now young adults but their devotion to him had remained constant since they were babies. Phoebe had felt that too, with her grandparents. That jump of a generation seemed to bypass the usual family *Sturm und Drang*, and thank God for that.

Dusk had fallen. Mandy got up to draw the curtains. She was in charge now, and thank God for that too. Phoebe certainly didn't resent this, not yet. She just marvelled at the vastness of Mandy's bottom in those silver leggings, worn no doubt to celebrate the occasion. Only a month had passed and she seemed to have put on even more weight. Though voluminous, her multicoloured sweater still bulged with her girth.

Their father, by contrast, had dwindled into a frail old man – still pretty attractive, with that thick head of hair – but with pitifully skinny arms ending in those liver-spotted hands, one of which Alice was still stroking.

The conversation had moved on to cuckoos. Warblers, it seemed, were the most common victims of the cuckoos' invasion. The female cuckoo pushed out the little warbler eggs and laid her own. The interloper hatched and grew vast, sitting there on its great bottom, dwarfing the frail warbler who had no idea what was happening to it.

'Ugh, gross!' said Alice.

Their father shrugged. 'Who knows if the warbler even notices?'

Mandy beamed at them. 'Time for cake!'

'I did like your outfit this morning,' Mandy said to Farida. 'Does it stop at the waist?'

Farida nodded. 'Of course. Below that I'm just wearing knickers.'

'Farida!' said Robert.

'She's joking,' said Alice. 'Don't listen to her.'

Mandy scooped some cream off her plate. 'I never used to listen to the news, it was always so horrible. But now I'm living here we watch it every day, don't we, love?' She popped her finger into her mouth and sucked it. 'Your father's trying to educate me.'

'And vice versa,' said the old man. 'Have you watched something called *Pointless*?'

'No,' said Robert.

'Yes,' said his daughter.

'It's a game show,' he said. 'Utterly hilarious. I didn't know who the people were but Mandy explained them to me. They seem to be celebrities just because they've been on other game shows a lot like this one. Something almost Nietzschean about it – the *Übermensch* and the doctrine of eternal return.'

'We're also into box sets,' said Mandy. '*Game of Thrones* is our favourite. We're on Series Three.'

'It's a riot,' said Dad. 'Wall-to-wall sex and violence. Why didn't I know about it before?' He turned to Mandy. 'Hopelessly addicted, aren't we, love?'

Love? It was odd hearing these new words coming out of their father's mouth. But he looked so happy, the birthday boy, *eighty-five years young*, as Mandy said.

Phoebe stole a glance at Farida, who was inspecting a chip in her nail varnish. She was in awe of Robert's wife – everyone was, to some extent. In Mandy's case it was because she was on the telly.

'Does she meet lots of stars?' she whispered to Phoebe later, in the kitchen.

'Not really. She trained as a journalist and knows about things, she has briefings and whatnot, but basically her job is to read the news.'

Mandy looked deflated. 'She's a bit old, though, isn't she?'

'Well, fifty-two.'

'They probably keep her on because they're supposed to do that.'

'Do what?'

'My friend Maureen says they're supposed to have older women on TV, and more Muslims.'

Phoebe looked at her sharply but Mandy, unperturbed, passed her a teacup to dry.

Phoebe felt another jolt – they all did – when Robert's family was preparing to leave. Jack said he had to be up early because he had to visit his friend Haydon, who was in Exeter Prison on drug offences. Jack said he was thinking of writing a letter to the *Guardian* about how many black men were banged up and what a scandal that was.

'Well, they do more crimes, don't they?' said Mandy.

There was a silence. Robert, one arm in his overcoat, swung round to look at her. 'What makes you say that?'

'They just do. Maybe you don't have any of them in Wimbledon but if you grew up where I did you'd know what I mean.'

A flurried leave-taking followed this.

As Phoebe drove home she wondered what her father thought about Mandy's views. He was a man of impeccable liberal credentials. When the SDP was formed in 1981 – how quaint and innocent those days seemed now! – he and her mother nearly came to blows over the split in the left wing and how they were going to vote. Now he was stuck twenty-four hours a day with a woman whose opinions would once have horrified him. But he'd said nothing. Did he not want to rock the boat? Phoebe knew why *she'd* stayed quiet – what if they'd had a row with Mandy and she left them in the lurch?

Or was he slipping into senility, where everything floated past in a thickening blur?

She was always on the lookout for any signs of dementia, her deepest fear. Dad was certainly becoming forgetful – the walls were stuck with Post-it notes, written by Mandy in big black letters: 'TEETH'. 'FLIES'. 'PILLS'. Most of the time Mandy was there to remind him, of course, but she'd recounted lurid stories she'd read in the *Daily Mail* about houses burning down because some old girl had forgotten to turn off the gas. Their dad hadn't started putting his wallet in the fridge but he did sometimes seem confused, and of course he kept forgetting people's names and where he'd left his specs. But then he'd always been pretty vague, the absent-minded professor; he'd relied on their mother for everything, from sorting out plumbers to remembering his children's birthdays.

Anyway, whatever his state of mind he was safe in Mandy's hands and they could breathe a sigh of relief. She might not have been his intellectual equal, and she certainly had some dubious views, but what the hell? She had become essential to their lives – to their father's, of course, most of all.

And from what they could tell she had become devoted to him. And he seemed devoted to her. She made it seem so easy.

Love ... beautiful love, unconditional love. We're born knowing it, and receiving it. And yet what messiness awaits us.

Phoebe's thing with Torren was still going on. Eighteen months and she still didn't know what to call it, though her brother had a word.

'Still seeing your fuckbuddy?' he asked. 'Aren't you a bit old for that sort of malarkey?'

Despite the sneer, Phoebe detected a note of envy. Only natural, when you'd been married as long as he had.

Torren lived in a hut in the middle of a wood a few miles out of town. He'd built it out of old doors, corrugated iron, mahogany panelling someone had thrown out, stuff he'd found in skips. It was rather charming. Inside it was carpeted with offcuts; there was a bed, mismatched chairs, a kitchen area with a Calor Gas stove. He had a generator for electricity. Even a rudimentary toilet. And masses of CDs, which he could play as loudly as he wanted, with nobody to disturb but the birds. Captain Beefheart, Grateful Dead.

There were plenty of old hippies around, in Phoebe's part of Wales. They'd migrated from London in the seventies and this was where they'd run out of petrol. So they'd stayed put, living in yurts and caravans and rotting Mercedes vans up in the hills, doing this and that, doing what they'd always done, and still smoking monster spliffs despite the condition of their teeth, or lack of them. You had to admire the stamina.

Torren was still handsome in a leathery sort of way. Dreadlocks, skinny body, a startling loud laugh and eyes that, like Mick Jagger's, twinkled with slightly suspect merriment. He was unusual in that he was born and bred in Wales and had inherited the wood from his uncle. At one point he'd tried to make a living growing blueberries, and the bushes could still be glimpsed, now engulfed by brambles. He'd had various other schemes but he didn't seem perturbed when they failed. In a clearing, there was still a tattered polytunnel from his days as the local drugs lord, but it was now choked with nettles. There was some hydro-electric scheme, long abandoned, which consisted of a dam and various lengths of plastic piping. But as he lived off-grid he didn't have to earn much money and survived on the odd carpentry job. Phoebe had no idea what he did all day. In this sense he resembled her brother.

She knew what Robert was supposed to be doing in *his* hut, of course: writing his novel. But what did he actually *do*? Three years was a long time with nothing to show for it. She knew it was set in her part of the world. When prodded, Robert said it was volume one of his Radnorshire Trilogy. He wouldn't be drawn, however, on what it was about. Phoebe suspected gnarled farmers and a lot of Welsh

Wuthering. That Robert lived in a multimillion-pound house in Wimbledon was neither here nor there, such is the power of the novelist's imagination. And Robert did have some connection to the place. Only twenty miles away, towards Crickhowell, was where they had spent summers in their holiday cottage. This countryside had powerful atavistic memories for him, as it had for Phoebe. It was the reason she had returned here to live, drawn back to Wales by the siren call of her childhood.

In January Phoebe had a phone call from her brother. 'You know your friend Torren?'

'Yes.'

'I wonder if you could do me a favour.'

'What sort of favour?'

'Ask him for some help.'

'Help?'

'It's about my novel.'

'Hmm . . . I've been wondering about that.'

'What do you mean?' he snapped.

'Just . . . I was wondering how it was getting on.'

'It's getting on fine!'

'I'm so glad.'

'Once you have the characters, you see, once you know them as well as I do, living with them day after day, they start to write it themselves.'

'That must be great.'

'It's like, *they're* telling *me* their story.' Robert's voice quickened. 'V. S. Pritchett said there's no such thing as plot, only characters. Once they've become living, breathing human beings, you see, you leave it up to them. You don't have to be frightened that you haven't got a story because they *are* the story.' He paused. 'If they're interesting enough.'

'And yours are interesting?'

'God, yes.'

He stopped, breathing heavily. Phoebe was pleased for him, of course. If he made a success of this, his pride would be restored. His wife might even – God forbid – treat him with some kind of respect instead of the usual borderline contempt.

'The thing is,' he said, 'I'm having a slight problem with what they actually *say*. My characters.'

'Ah.'

'Of course, I know what they *mean* to say. I just don't know how they put it into words.'

It turned out that they all spoke in nineteenth-century Radnorshire dialect. That was the problem. Torren, born and bred in the area, might be able to help.

'If I send you a list, perhaps you could give it to him? He could translate it into Radnorshire-ese or whatever they call it. I'm sure it hasn't changed much over the years. I've got to make it sound authentic.'

There was a note of desperation in his voice that touched Phoebe. She said she'd give it a go.

'Thanks, sis,' he said. 'You're a star.'

The next day she drove up to Tan-y-Wynt, Torren's wood. It was in a steep valley and in the winter months plunged permanently in shadow. It was still beautiful, however, always beautiful, a secret cleft in the world filled with ancient trees furred with moss. She had Little Feat playing, full volume, and sang along to 'Feel The Groove'.

Funnily enough, she was looking forward to her task. It

gave her a reason to visit Torren, and something for them to talk about. Their relationship, if she could call it that, had somewhat stagnated. Her visits to his hut were so disconnected from her normal life – that was the problem. They were a one-night stand, multiplied many times, with no continuity and nothing to grow from. She sometimes saw Torren in Costcutter buying a bottle of vodka but they had no friends in common, no common ground. No conversation, to be perfectly honest.

Oh, there was talk, plenty of that. But it was he who did the talking while Phoebe sat on the floor, wedged between his legs, gazing at the flames of his log-burner. In the beginning she found this liberating. It reminded her of her past; she was young again, being lectured on extra-terrestrials by some stoned stranger with whom she'd just had sex. In fact, to be perfectly honest, she sometimes wondered if she only persevered with this sort of *malarkey* to prove that she could still do it. Catch other women her age traipsing out to a rotting hut just to get laid! This might sound smug but what the hell? It beat the Defibrillator Awareness Evening at the Memorial Hall.

They'd met when she was struggling through the bracken in what turned out to be his wood. She'd lost her way and was trying to get back to the road. He stood in a clearing – a skinny, wild-looking man, digging a hole.

'Looking for something?' he asked.

'I don't know,' she replied. 'Am I?'

She was not usually so Zen; blame it on his dreadlocks. He didn't seem to mind her trespassing, anyway, and told her he'd just seen an otter.

This was thrilling, of course, so he led her down to the

stream and they sat there, waiting for it to reappear. He said the water was the purest in Wales so she scooped up some and drank. He banged on for a while about lichens, how many varieties grew in his wood due to the lack of pollution, but she wasn't listening. It was a drowsy day in midsummer; nature was sunk in torpor and she couldn't be bothered to exert herself. The bank rose up steeply on the other side of the stream. It was crowded with hart's-tongue ferns – shiny straps, brilliantly green. She said she was an artist and would love to paint them, so Torren said come back any time.

And she did. The very next day, in fact. Scrambling down the bank, she set up her easel and started work. Torren knew she was there because she'd parked her car near his hut, but she didn't see him for hours. All she heard was the sound of an axe, and later on some music.

Then something crashed through the undergrowth. A dog tore down the bank and shoved its nose up her skirt.

It was some sort of mongrel, matted and shapeless, the sort of dog that looks the same back to front. A patch of fur had been shaved off, revealing pink skin and a row of stitches.

Torren appeared and sat down on a tree root.

'Nice dog,' she lied.

'Had a tumour in his spine, poor fucker,' he said. 'They kept him in for three days and he nearly tore the place apart.' The dog withdrew its head from her crotch and Torren gave it a stroke. 'Nice one, Ziggy.'

He started rolling a spliff. As he did so she thought of the last time she'd had sex. It was, humiliatingly, eight years earlier. She had a suspicion that quite soon she might be having it with Torren. There was something about the way he lounged there, presumptuously eyeing her bare legs, that seemed promising.

The industrial-strength skunk helped. Phoebe hadn't smoked dope for years and though she knew it had mutated into something more powerful she had no idea what it would do to her brain and indeed her inhibitions. They somehow got to his hut and onto his disordered bed. God knew when he had last washed the sheets; luckily the light was fading so she couldn't see them clearly – more to the point, he couldn't see *her* clearly as she pulled off her clothes with what she hoped was careless abandon. Mind you, he was no spring chicken either and gratifyingly spongey around the midriff.

So there she was, naked in bed with a naked man. The first moment was painful, like pushing open a rusty door on a long-disused shop. She'd read about this problem with older women but hadn't put it to the test. He took it slowly, however – he was surprisingly considerate – and soon lust took over and their bodies were moving together in that miraculous conversation she thought she would never have again, the dog nipping their toes until Torren kicked him out.

Afterwards they both burst out laughing. It was a lovely moment, that – the laughter. Phoebe was young again. *Young.*

That was how it started. As the months passed, however, she realised Torren knew nothing about her life and indeed expressed no interest in it. She didn't mind, it was not as if they were friends, but it did seem somewhat lopsided when he'd told her so much about himself, so she was looking forward to something more resembling a conversation.

It was raining when she turned off the road. Torren had erected a sculpture at the entrance to his wood: a driftwood totem pole, stuck with nitrous oxide capsules and topped with a sheep's skull. She drove down the track, tyres skidding in the mud. Now it was winter, various objects were revealed, rotting in the undergrowth – the carcass of a rowing boat, a pile of motorbike entrails, the skeleton of an ancient caravan, blackened with mould. As usual, Phoebe felt pleasantly lawless. Imagine Farida here! Imagine her face!

Torren's dog no longer barked at her arrival. She considered this a sign of acceptance. Outside the hut lay a dead rabbit, its head bitten off; sometimes Ziggy brought her his victims and dropped them at her feet, an act that she found strangely flattering even though the bearer was so repulsive.

The rabbit, wet and matted, lay there like an empty glove. *Bye, baby Bunting, Daddy's gone a'hunting. Gone to fetch a rabbit skin, to wrap the baby Bunting in.* When she was little Phoebe loved that nursery rhyme; it made her feel safe. Her father was so affectionate, like the father in the song, but then he too kept leaving – not hunting, in his case, but disappearing into an unknowable adult world of Conferences and Abroad.

Torren came out of his hut and hugged her. He smelled pleasingly of roll-ups and wood smoke.

'I bet your father went hunting,' Phoebe said. 'The real thing, rabbits and crows and whatnot.' It wasn't far away, the farm where he was brought up – just over the hill towards Llandrigg.

'Yeah.' He sat down, groaning. His arthritis was playing up. 'Bloody rain, bloody Wales.'

'You should have got used to it by now.'

He took out a bottle of cloudy liquid. 'Been drinking this to numb the pain.'

It was some sort of hooch. He said his mate Bendicks made it by hanging up marrows and draining them through ladies' tights. Torren poured some into a mug and passed it to her. 'Eighty per cent proof; it'll knock your socks off.'

He said that Bendicks lived in a showman's wagon in the next valley and had been in and out of gaol.

'Why's he called Bendicks?' she asked. 'Is it some old Welsh name?'

Torren shook his head. ''Cos that's what he stole.'

'Bendicks Bittermints?'

'Pardon?'

'I don't blame him,' she said. 'They're delicious.'

'No, sweetheart. Bendix. The washing machines.'

'Goodness. Aren't they a bit heavy?'

'Not if you got a five-ton lorry.'

'Still, seems an awful lot of effort.'

He shrugged. 'He's a nutter. When we were in Amsterdam, back in the day, we went on this massive bender. First we dropped some acid, then we went for the magic mushrooms and his brain, like, exploded. So he's jumping into the canals and freaking out . . .'

Phoebe drifted off. Once Torren started on these legendary acid trips it could go on for ages, as meandering as a Norse Saga and just as incomprehensible.

She took a sip. The hooch tasted like battery fluid. She decided to stop Torren mid-flow and ask him Robert's questions, otherwise there wouldn't be time for a fuck before her choral group. They were practising 'Thanks for the Memory'. Now that *was* romantic, so wonderfully romantic it made her swoon. She felt a lurch of sadness that Torren would never sing that about her. Nor, indeed, would she sing it about him.

'I've got a brother who's writing a book about Radnorshire,' she said. 'I know it's called Powys now, but his book is set a hundred years ago when it was still the old name.' She rummaged in her bag. 'It's a trilogy, apparently.'

'A what?'

'But he's only on volume one.' She found a sheet of paper and passed it to him. 'Seeing as your family has been farming here for ages, he wondered if you could help him with some words.'

Torren looked startled. He held the paper at a distance, as if it might explode. She realised he was pretty drunk.

'Could you do it?' she asked. 'Translate them into dialect?'

'No problemo.'

He blinked, gathering his wits. Phoebe sat down beside him and pointed out the words. *Wind, rain, sleet, snow, virgin, still-birth, epileptic fit, umbilical cord, castration, axe, seizure, death . . .*

'Sounds like a laugh a minute,' said Torren.

Each word had a space next to it, for Torren her fuck-buddy to fill in.

The word *fuckbuddy* still annoyed her. Only a brother could be so contemptuous. On the other hand she was grateful to him for tasking her with this project and introducing another element into her whatever-it-was-called, her *thing*, with Torren. In future, she decided, she would call it an *off-grid relationship* – disconnected from the mains of emotional dependency. That was an improvement.

Torren put on his specs; the first time she'd seen him wearing any. Instantly he looked more intelligent. Borrowing her biro, he started scribbling down the dialect translations, word by word.

Phoebe was astonished at his speed. 'Wow, you know them all?'

'Most of 'em. My nan, my dad, they all spoke this shit.'

She looked at his scrawl: *withmass, llanslab, sythe, curmudden*. 'What a beautiful language,' she said.

'Normal for me, doll,' he replied, still scribbling away. He finished with a flourish and grabbed her. 'Now let's get those panties off.'

Half an hour later Phoebe drove back up the track. The light was fading and the rain had stopped. Sex hadn't been so painful this time; it seemed the pessaries were working. But then there was the dreaded cystitis, which was almost worse. Her father said, *Old age is not for cissies,* but the same could be said for being a woman, especially a woman of sixty. The only positive thing was that she couldn't get pregnant. Gone were the days when she fumbled with her diaphragm in some pub toilet, hands slippery with spermicidal jelly and, on one occasion, catapulting the blasted thing across the room. Not to mention the torture of having a coil inserted. How undignified are the foundations for rapture, and how dearly bought! Men have no idea.

Phoebe was thinking this as she turned onto the road and started driving down the hill. A car appeared, approaching from the opposite direction. It looked familiar, and she realised it belonged to her neighbour Pam, a matronly quilt-maker.

Pam passed her and for some reason Phoebe glanced in the rear-view mirror. Maybe she suspected something, who knows?

For Pam's brakes lights came on. Then her indicator winked left, and she drove into Torren's wood.

Robert

There were two women in his life who scared Robert. One was his sister and the other was his wife. They both knew him too well, that was the problem. Such different women, so vastly different, but they had this in common. That narrow-eyed look, their heads tilted sideways – he knew, of course, what they were inspecting. It was him. *Him*. The naked, cowering, cringingly inadequate human being, still curled in a foetal ball.

The children were different because he was their dad. However much they might complain, a dad's a fully formed adult. He's the constant; it's *they* who have the licence to change and grow, and change and grow they must. But they simply had no idea, no idea at all.

Robert was mulling over this as he took his afternoon walk. He missed his dog – still, after all this time. Without Bismarck on the lead his arm hung as useless as a flipper. He missed those moist brown eyes and unconditional love. Bismarck saw right into his quivering soul but unlike Robert's nearest and dearest he remained utterly devoted.

Did everyone feel this way? That if somebody cut them open they'd be appalled at what they found? He couldn't ask Farida; she'd dismiss it as the self-indulgent blathering of someone with too much time on his hands. His sister would be equally dismissive. She'd blame it on their parents but claim that she'd been more damaged than him, that he'd been the favoured one because he was the first-born, and a boy. It would bring *that* old chestnut up again. If anything, their rivalry had worsened over the years.

When he'd mentioned this to Farida she just said, *Grow up*. She gave short shrift to middle-class neurosis. She'd inherited this toughness from her father. Salim was a self-made businessman who'd spent his childhood running errands in Bohri Bazaar and ended up owning the largest clothing factory in Karachi. Robert had never liked him and Salim had never liked Robert; he considered him a wimp, too spineless to take care of his daughter. After his expulsion from the City, Salim had become openly contemptuous and even Farida had had to stick up for her husband. How different was Salim from his own father, that gentle charmer! But then his father had always had it easy. Bookish parents, private school, nannies and dogs, top marks everywhere, that privileged upbringing that those who enjoyed it so totally took for granted.

The challenge was to get some of this into his book. Cross-currents, resentments, inadequacies, parental guilt, naked terror – in other words, normal family life. Robert's characters scraped a living on a smallholding in the wilds of Wales. Their days were spent in snowdrifts, pulling blood-matted lambs out of ewes, battling the elements, slaughtering bullocks, being trampled by runaway horses. Would they have *time* for all this family stuff, or indeed the vocabulary for it? Plus they lived a hundred years ago, which didn't make it any easier. To be perfectly honest, he didn't really have a clue what they were feeling at all. To admit this, however, was to surrender to panic.

Thank God, therefore, for Phoebe's wild man of the woods. Robert had never set eyes on the chap but he'd delivered the goods and for that he was deeply grateful. Because Torren had released his characters from their permafrost. The words started pouring from their mouths ... *sythe*, *glantish*, *curmudden*, *glancrockit* ... They rolled around Robert's tongue and onto his keyboard, visceral and earthy, filled with the stench of reality. They lifted his plodding prose and galvanised it. At last his farming family had sprung to life, cursing and cackling, stomping through the mud – the *kekkle* – and at last, at long last, telling him their story. One event was leading to another with a momentum that was thrillingly out of his control. This is what novelists felt! Before, he'd been fooling myself. Now, miraculously, it had become a reality. In the mornings he could hardly wait to get to his shed and fling open his laptop. No nap, either. In the past week he'd written 3,456 words. That was 3,267 more than he'd written in the whole of January.

'You're writing a book?' asked Mandy. 'That must be interesting. Help yourself to salad.'

'I believe it's set in Wales,' said his father. 'We used to have a cottage there.'

'Yes, love, I know.' Mandy gave Robert a wink. His dad had probably told her about the cottage, many times. The repetitions were getting worse.

'You could see the Black Mountains from the bedroom window,' said his father. 'At dusk, the bats streamed from the barn. The children ran free all day long.'

'You don't have to go to Wales for a story,' said Mandy.

'Some of the people here, you should write a book about *them.*'

His father turned to him: 'Did you know that Graham, next door, has no kidneys?'

'Not even *one*,' said Mandy. 'That's how he met his lady friend.'

'He was having his dialysis, you see, and this woman came into the renal unit by mistake—'

'She was looking for her goddaughter—' said Mandy.

'– who'd just given birth to twins,' said his dad, 'but nobody knew who the father was, though some people suspected a chap who'd installed her solar panels. Anyway, Janet recognised Graham – it turned out they'd met on some package holiday when they were both married to somebody else – and bingo!'

'She said it was like she'd known him all her life.'

'Isn't that amazing?' said his dad. 'All these years and I'd had about three conversations with them. Mostly about that blasted Jack Russell.'

Robert watched him attack his corned beef. It was early in February and he'd driven down for lunch. Phoebe said she was worried about their dad but he couldn't see why. The old man seemed in fine fettle. Frail, of course, and sometimes confused, but the chap *was* eighty-five. He could shuffle around the house and get in and out of the car. The steep, narrow stairs were now out of bounds but he seemed quite cheerful about that. Pointing at Mandy, he said: 'She could be keeping a family of Romanians up there, and blessed if I'd know.'

'And their pig,' she said.

They both chuckled. Robert gazed at Mandy sitting there,

bathed in the sunshine that shafted through the window. She'd had her hair cut short, pudding-basin style. It was almost wilfully hideous; with that doughy face she bore a strong resemblance to Tweedledum. Or, indeed, Tweedledee. But on that winter's day she was dear to him. She had given Dad a new lease of life, and Robert certainly had no qualms about her, none at all.

A faint chirrup came from the kitchen. The great tit: two o'clock. Mandy cleared away the plates and brought in three mousses in individual pots: chocolate, strawberry and banana.

'Your dad and I can never decide which we like best so we toss for it,' she said.

Robert watched them squabbling playfully. Just for a moment he felt envious. It might be infantile but they were having a lark. A hoot.

'I know!' exclaimed his father. 'We'll all have a spoonful from each other's pots. Robert, being the outsider, can judge which is the best. His decision is final.'

Mandy said they bought the mousses at Lidl in Cirencester. 'It's our weekly treat, isn't it, Pops? We've got our favourite cashier, she's called Dympnia. She's got a child with learning disabilities. She says her job's her lifeline.'

Lunch was over and his father suggested moving to the window where two armchairs had been wedged side by side. It was here that he and Mandy watched the birds. His enthusiasm was infectious and she was now an expert. A notebook lay on the table where they wrote down the different species: fifteen so far. Various bird-feeders hung from the branches of the apple tree – niger seeds for finches, peanuts for tits.

'They come in from the fields because there's nothing for them to eat there,' said Mandy. 'The big farm's been bought by someone Chinese and wildlife is low on their list of priorities. They'd *eat* the birds if they had a chance. After all, they eat everything else, don't they? Dogs and things.'

She said the Chinese owned the pub, too. The Foreign Secretary had been Instagrammed eating lunch there with some Chinese trade minister and the picture had winged around the world. Exports of the local beer had soared.

'They like our Royal Family, you see,' Mandy said, tucking a blanket around the old man's knees. 'British customs, bangers and mash.'

'How do you know all this?' Robert asked.

'Bianka told me. She works behind the bar. She's from Hungary but they're almost like us, aren't they? She said the old owner went bankrupt because there's a supermodel who comes down at weekends and she kept booking a table for Sunday lunch, like for thirty people, then not turning up. All that good food gone to waste. So he's thrown in the towel and gone to live in Spain. His wife stayed behind because she's become a lesbian. She's got a job at the riding stables.'

Robert was impressed. He had no idea all this was happening and nor, he was sure, had his dad. The village had seemed pretty boring to him.

'I told you, somebody should put it in a book,' she said.

Suddenly his own novel seemed pitifully dull and irrelevant. Why should anyone be remotely interested in hoary old sheep-shaggers a hundred years ago?

Mandy tapped his knee. 'But I'm sure yours will be ever so interesting.' He jumped. Had she read his thoughts? 'You're brainy, like your dad.'

She retired to the kitchen to do the washing-up, leaving him alone with his father.

They sat there for a while in silence.

'Mandy's certainly made herself at home here,' Robert said. 'In the village.'

'You bet. She's a people person.'

Robert looked at him. *People person?* But then he was using all sorts of new words nowadays.

'I'm so glad you're getting along,' Robert said. 'You and Mandy. The other two were such a disaster.'

'We do, we do! She was devoted to her parents, you know, utterly devoted. She was an only child and very much loved. When they died she was devastated.' He settled deeper into his chair. 'I think she sees me as a sort of father substitute. And that's fine by me.'

At the bottom of the garden stood a line of poplar trees, their branches lacy-bare, their trunks trousered with ivy. They cast their long shadows across the lawn, which was dusted with frost. *That's fine by me.* Of course it was. By Robert, too.

Simpler, of course, to be a substitute; simpler than the real thing.

'Fancy a martini?' asked his dad.

'What, now?'

'Why not?' He turned round and bellowed, 'Mandy!'

Mandy seemed perfectly amenable, though she wasn't a drinker herself. Robert heard the fridge door open and the rattle of ice-cubes, then she carried in the tray and two glasses. His father insisted on mixing the cocktails himself. His hand trembled, however, as he poured out the martinis. Robert leaned over to help but Mandy got there first. As her fingers folded over his, steadying him, she glanced at Robert. Was it a look of triumph, that she was the carer and now in charge? Or was it a look of collusion, that they both had to humour an old man and his eccentric demands? She wasn't like anyone Robert knew; he hadn't a clue.

'Tomorrow's a big day, isn't it, pet?' said Mandy, popping an olive into his glass.

'We're going to the Kidderminster Retail Park,' said his dad.

'Last week we went to Bicester Village,' she said.

'What an eye-opener *that* was,' said the old man. 'Have you heard of it? Streets and streets of shops in the middle of nowhere—'

'Burberry, Gucci, all the designer outlets—'

'We don't buy anything, of course—'

'Just window-shop,' said Mandy. 'And people-watch.'

'They pour in there, coachloads of them: Japanese, Poles, they come to England *especially to go there*. It's most extraordinary.'

Mandy nudged him. 'Be honest, what you *really* like is your lunch at Nando's. Tell Robbie what you like best.'

'Peri-Peri Chicken Wings,' said his father.

'With chilli jam.'

'With chilli jam.' He indicated Mandy. 'She's a wimp and just has a burger.'

Mandy giggled and cracked open a Pepsi. The two men clinked glasses and drank. Dad was right, of course. Martinis after lunch, who cared? He might die tomorrow. But Robert was starting to worry about his state of mind. That Rolls-Royce of a brain seemed to be dwindling into discussions about retail outlets and chocolate mousse. Was it due to the company he kept, or was it simply an inevitable part of the ageing process? Whatever the cause, he seemed perfectly happy, and that was a cause of celebration. And, indeed, a martini.

'*Dad*, at *Bicester Village*?' Phoebe gasped. 'You must be joking.'

'He said he had a high old time.'

'Doing what?'

'Hanging out.'

'*Hanging out?*'

'Looking at the shops.'

'*What?*'

'That's what he said.'

'But it's a ghastly place. Like a Dantesque limbo of Purgatory.'

'Have you ever been?'

'No! Of course not.' She paused. 'And he hates clothes. He's always worn just any old thing. And Mum bought him those, anyway.'

'They went to Nando's.'

Phoebe burst out laughing. 'No way!'

'I know, I know,' Robert replied. 'He seems to be becoming a completely different person.'

There was a silence. He could sense Phoebe, down the line, considering this. 'What's she doing to him?'

The question startled him. He didn't realise, till then, that he'd been thinking exactly the same thing.

Later, Robert thought about this conversation. Maybe he and Phoebe were being patronising. Why should they sneer

at something just because they didn't want to do it themselves? If, with Mandy, he was living another sort of
life – well, bully for him. And bully for Mandy. She had a
right to enjoy herself. It couldn't be easy, stuck in the middle of nowhere in the middle of winter with a marginally
incontinent old man with a fund of repetitive stories about
people she'd never known. Cutting his toenails and taking
him to the doctor. Bathing him and dressing him. Getting
up in the small hours to help him to the toilet. Cooking and
cleaning for him. Massaging his cold grey corpse's feet.

Neither Robert nor his sister was doing this. They had
absolved themselves of responsibility by paying somebody
else. So who were they to judge?

Phoebe

By now, Phoebe knew a little about Mandy's life – an only child, loving parents, father a postman. Mandy talked a lot about her friend Maureen but made it plain it wasn't *like that*. She'd had several boyfriends, apparently, long ago when she was still a size twelve, and told Phoebe details of these relationships with a certain combative frankness, as if to prove that she too had had a past. She talked about her early years in various jobs and how she'd found her vocation when helping out with an elderly neighbour. 'I was changing his dressing,' she said, 'and something clicked.'

But it was Dad who Phoebe talked to, on her visits. That was the reason she went there, after all. Mandy would be bustling about in the background, or nipping out to run an errand. She prattled on about this and that but half the time Phoebe wasn't listening.

For, to be perfectly honest, she found her boring.

Besides, she had other preoccupations. For a start, her work wasn't going well. Nobody was buying it, that was the trouble; the market was saturated. *More bloody sheep,* she could hear people thinking. Not a single red sticker had appeared on her exhibition at the surgery. She'd packed up her paintings in silence, surrounded by patients who sat there gazing into the middle distance, absorbed with their own possibly mortal symptoms while Pachelbel played on an endless loop. Who could blame them?

That didn't stop her wanting to give them a shake. *I'm here!* she'd shouted silently. *I exist!*

But it was deeper than that. She was certainly competent but strangely enough that was the problem. Her cow parsley remained just that: cow parsley. It hadn't been magicked into something beyond itself. A year earlier she had made a solitary pilgrimage to Bruges. Whipped by the wind, she had trudged from the Groeninge Museum to the Memling Museum, studying the Flemish masters. How did they do it? There was Van Eyck, making humble sparrows sing. Memling, making lilies trumpet into life for the glory of God, the glory of every human being. Their beauty transfixed her. She stood in the empty museum, the only sound the *click-click* as the attendant sat in the corner cutting his fingernails.

Fail well. Fail again. Fail better. But she wasn't exactly failing; that was the problem.

Then there was the threat to her town. That's how some of them saw it, anyway. Lidl wanted to build a supermarket on an old factory site, next to the council estate, and people feared it would kill the High Street. Since the news Phoebe had gazed at the shops with pity, like someone who'd been told of a cancer diagnosis of which the patient was still unaware ... The butcher's, the hardware store, Audrey's with its dusty mannequin, her wig askew. The greengrocer's where, if Emlyn had run out of parsley, he said, *There's some in my garden, love, just go and pick it.* Winnie's Newsagents with its small ad for *Half a ton of manure, buyer collects.* These shops were the heart of the community and one of the reasons she had come to live in Knockton.

It was stirring up divisions in the town – the class divisions she'd thought more or less non-existent in her rural backwater. The lower-income families would love a Lidl (so, come to think of it, would Mandy and Dad). Those people who were protesting against it – well, a lot of them were incomers, weren't they? Arty, beardie, lefty, probably with a bob or two. It was all getting pretty heated.

Then there was Torren. She'd always had her suspicions, of course, that she wasn't the only woman who visited his little hut. Despite the prostate problem he was still game; she'd glimpsed a packet of Viagra behind his frying pan. Besides, why shouldn't he be? They weren't married. They weren't anything.

That was the logical response, but who said sex had anything to do with anything that remotely resembled *anything* remotely resembling logic? The sight of Pam's car had triggered an unwelcome image that Phoebe couldn't shake off: a succession of lonely, middle-aged women arriving for their weekly service. Oiling the plugs and so on. It all got rather disgusting after that.

She'd seen signs of visitors, of course. Female ones. An invitation to the Cross-stitch Extravaganza in the Assembly Rooms (no fear); the remains of a Bakewell tart in a dish she recognised as belonging to Poppy, a local sculptress; a Chanel lipstick (nobody Phoebe knew, not in Knockton). Then there was *The Colour Purple*, wedged in Torren's shelf between *Growing Soft Fruit* and *Selected Lyrics of Bob Dylan* – either a gift from a feminist hoping to radicalise him (fat chance) or somebody who'd stayed long enough to read a book.

Though unsettled by this spoor, Phoebe was also

strangely gratified. Judging by the evidence, Torren seemed to go for women of his own vintage. How seldom was this the case! Most men she knew had copped off with a younger model – in some cases, practically in nappies. How ridiculous this was, when the chaps might soon be in nappies themselves.

But it was still disturbing. Through various conversations she'd gathered that Torren had a bit of a rep – what healthy, single, heterosexual man didn't? But she was starting to comprehend the number of women involved.

She decided to confide in her friend Monica, a brittle, neurotic woman who had recently married a man called Buffy. He was the veteran of several marriages and many liaisons. Rumour had it that when he was in Soho, his old stamping ground, he used to pat the heads of passing children in case one of them was his. Monica, surely, would have learned how to cope with that most humiliating and counterproductive of emotions, jealousy?

'No fucking way,' she said.

She and Buffy ran the Myrtle House Hotel, further down the High Street. Phoebe was sitting in the kitchen. She liked entering the swing door marked 'Staff Only'; it felt mildly transgressive.

'I used to think of all those women,' Monica said, 'and whether they were better at it than me. I used to torture myself by picturing them, and thinking that whatever he was doing he had done it a thousand times before.' She sloshed more wine into their glasses. 'I used to think I've shared this body with so many other people it's hardly mine at all. I know it's stupid – who am *I* to talk – but it's not rational, is it?'

'No.'

'So it's not so funny with you and Mr Dreadlocks. It's just so utterly, coruscatingly painful to think of them with somebody else. Anybody else. Even if you hardly love them at all. Which you don't seem to do. Do you?'

The back door opened and Buffy came in, stamping his feet from the cold.

'Hello, Phoebe! What are you talking about, anything interesting?'

'Lidl,' said Monica. 'The campaign strategy.'

'I'll be off then.' He hurried out, the swing door sighing.

'He wouldn't be interested anyway,' Phoebe said. 'Being a bloke.'

'Don't be ridiculous.' Monica rolled her eyes. 'He'd be absolutely riveted. We talk about relationships all day long.'

Suddenly desolated, Phoebe gazed at the row of saucepans hanging above the cooker. Their bottoms were scorched from years of use. Nobody wanted to embark on marriage with her – the long haul, the launch into the dark, the chats and squabbles and foolish, retrospective jealousies. The talking about relationships all day long, if you were lucky enough to be Monica, and married to a man who liked that sort of thing. All Phoebe was good for was a fumble in a shed. How undignified was that?

Monica gave her a level look. 'You're beautiful, Phoebe, and funny, and talented—'

'I'm *so* not.'

'Shut up! Your problem is low self-esteem. Where on earth does *that* come from?'

Draining her glass, Phoebe thought of her father. So

warm and charming, so beloved by everyone, yet somehow never there when she was growing up, and needed him. Always called away, always on the phone, always getting into a taxi to go somewhere more interesting than the place where she happened to be.

Her parents bought Hafod when she and Robert were children. It was a remote cottage near the Black Mountains and it always took longer than expected to get there. Wales was like that; everywhere was further than you thought. Even when they finally turned off the road there was still a mile to go, up a winding track with cattle grids. The nearest town, Crickhowell, was ten miles away, and during the first year the cottage didn't even have a phone.

Phoebe could still feel the rush of joy when she stumbled out of the car. Oh, the rapture of being six, the summer holidays stretching into infinity! It was probably raining but who cared? She and Robert were free. And they had their parents to themselves.

Not that they bothered with them. One whole summer they spent rolling tyres down a hill. They poked sticks into the crust of cowpats and dammed the stream. Basically, they just mucked about. But they knew he was there, their father, and nobody could get at him.

He certainly seemed pretty contented. He said the place was heaven on earth and sat beside the fire reciting poetry to them while their mother wrestled with the Raeburn in the kitchen. She did most of the chores. Whether she was resentful about this didn't cross their minds. They were children; they didn't think that way. Dad's efforts to be practical were a family joke and they presumed, then, that she simply indulged him. They remembered him wearing, for reasons best known to himself, brown overalls like a Pickford's removal man. He'd wander around the cottage, prodding at the dry rot and *tssking* through his teeth, then do nothing about it. His attempt at unblocking the sink resulted in a legendary flood, and his gardening was restricted to stabbing ineffectually at the weeds that grew around the back door, still within earshot of the Home Service.

He was known locally as the Nutty Professor. In those days their neighbours were mostly farmers and regarded him with affectionate bemusement. There was none of the animosity towards English weekenders that was around at the time. It was just another tribute to his charm.

There was another reason Phoebe was so happy there. Buying Hafod coincided with Dad finding her more interesting. Mostly, in fact, it was him talking but she didn't mind, she was being treated as an equal. A sounding-board, really, for his idle musings.

'I've been thinking about dogs,' he said as they lay on the grass. 'A walk for them is another map completely, a map of a million smells. How superior to us! And yet they can only bark. While the budgie is lower down the scale but, how amazing, a budgie can talk! Apparently there's a budgie called Puck who can speak 1,728 words. And why do we rate both those creatures above flies, whose eyes have 6,000 little lenses so they can see movement all round? *And* another eye in between, which works as their compass? Yet we swat them without a thought. Make sense of *that*, my chickadee.'

'Flies are bottom of the heap because they eat poo,' she said.

'So do dogs.'

They both burst out laughing. He lay there gazing at her, his head propped in his hand. 'I'm so glad you're six and we can have a proper conversation.'

His hair was dark, then, wild and wiry. He wasn't exactly handsome, even she could see that, but very dear. Loose, generous features, a face that creased deliciously when he smiled – which he did, a lot. A greed for life and a startling laugh that could make passers-by jump. Phoebe was so proud to be seen with him, not because he was distinguished – she knew nothing about that – but because he lit up those around him and made everything fun.

Hafod, and their life in Wales, came up in a conversation with Mandy. It was a chilly day in March and Phoebe had driven down for lunch. She was feeling guilty that she hadn't visited for a month but when she arrived her father looked the picture of contentment. He was sitting in his armchair, blanket over his knees, listening to *Tristram Shandy* on his headphones and scraping away at a scratchcard. He'd caught the gambling bug from Mandy and they were addicted to the lottery, tuning in to the telly when the results were announced. 'The high spot of our day, isn't it, Mandy?'

There was something different about the room. It took Phoebe a moment to spot it. White cotton bibs, edged with lace, were now draped over the back of the armchairs. The arm-rests, too. Antimacassars! A word that had never passed her lips.

'We bought them in Dunelm,' said Mandy, following her gaze. 'I hope you don't mind, but they'll save on those cleaning bills.'

Then Phoebe noticed a cream, fluffy hearthrug. Mandy said that on her day off she had gone up to Solihull and collected it from her parents' house, to replace the existing one, which was old and stained with scorch-marks. 'I haven't thrown it away, of course,' she said. 'It's in the cupboard under the stairs.'

Phoebe didn't mind, not at that stage. Her father certainly didn't, but then he'd never had any taste; that was her mother's department. The room just looked slightly less theirs – cosier, more suburban.

Over lunch they talked about Hafod. Her father told Mandy about the bats, yet again. Mandy responded as if this was new to her, nodding her head and encouraging him. This went with the job, of course. Phoebe remembered the story about Mrs Klein and her endless conversational loop. Mandy was paid to indulge her clients' foibles and needs, however wearily repetitive, and make it fresh each time – like a prostitute, thought Phoebe. Though anyone less like a prostitute would be hard to imagine.

Phoebe looked around the room. Mandy had put up net curtains in the front window to stop people peering in. It was becoming their home, Dad's and hers. The back view of the two armchairs, wedged together at the window, made this plain. His carer was his companion now. She might not be the person he would choose, in his prime, but he was an enfeebled old man and it was Mandy who was meeting his needs. Scratchcards and all.

After lunch, while he dozed in the living room, the two women did the washing-up. As so often happens, standing there side by side, engaged in a communal task, released confidences.

At first they chatted about Hafod.

'It sounds a lovely spot,' Mandy said.

'It was.'

'All the family together.'

'Yes, except Dad kept going away.' With sudden venom, Phoebe rubbed a knife dry. 'He said he'd be there for the summer and three days later he'd be gone.'

She opened the cutlery drawer and stopped. It was filled with tea towels.

'Knives and forks in there now.' Mandy pointed to another drawer. 'It's handier.'

Phoebe shoved them in with a clatter. She realised she was drunk from the white wine at lunch. 'He *promised*, you see. He promised we'd all be together. We had these trips planned – going to Aberystwyth, going canoeing. Then he'd get a phone call – God, how I hated that phone! – and we'd see the taxi coming up the hill to take him to the station.' Her voice rose, bitterly. 'That bloody taxi!'

'A man's gotta do what a man's gotta do.'

'What's *that* supposed to mean?'

Mandy shrugged. 'He probably had important work to do.'

'More important than *us*? We were his *children*!' Phoebe slammed the drawer shut. 'It was bad enough at home, in Oxford, him being away half the time, never being there for sports day, even when he *was* there not being there, being shut away in his study.' She paused for breath. 'But this was the *holidays*.'

Mandy pulled off her rubber gloves. 'How old are you, love?'

'Sixty.'

'Shouldn't you be over this by now?' Her voice was cold. 'I'm sorry, sweetheart, but I speak as I find. Haven't you got anything better to worry about?'

Phoebe was speechless. Mandy turned. Her glasses were steamed up. Phoebe couldn't read her expression.

'Nobody likes a Moaning Minnie.'

Mandy laid her rubber gloves side by side on the draining board and rested her hands on top of them, breathing heavily. Phoebe noticed, for the first time, that Mandy had bitten her fingernails down to the quick, the skin red and raw. For some reason this surprised her.

Then she did a funny thing. She butted Phoebe with her hip – a sort of playful nudge, as if they were heifers. Phoebe couldn't decide if she was moving her out of the way or indicating that she'd only been joking.

Then she pulled off her apron and left.

'I'm not sure about Mandy,' Phoebe said.

'What do you mean?' Robert's voice was sharp. 'What's happened?'

'Nothing really. She was rather sarky with me today and then she pretty well pushed me out of the house.'

'*Pushed* you?'

'She just said that as Dad was asleep didn't I want to get back home before it got dark? It *wasn't* dark, it was only half-past three.'

'That's all?'

'I suppose so.'

Phoebe heard a sigh. 'Aren't you being a little bit . . .'

'A bit what?'

'You know.'

'*What?*'

'Over-reactive?' He paused. 'I mean, you sometimes do this.'

'Do what?'

'Well, make a bit of a drama.'

'That's so unfair! I'm just *telling* you what I *felt*. She has this funny look in her eyes.'

'Well *I've* never noticed it. She seems a perfectly nice, rather boring woman to me. She might have some views we don't agree with but then so does half the country. We just never meet them.'

They finished their conversation. Phoebe's window was open; across the yard, in the back of the butcher's shop, she heard the *clunk-clunk* of the meat cleaver. Needless to say, Robert's tone annoyed her. He'd always done this: turning everything round, turning it into an attack.

She also suspected that he didn't want to rock the boat – anything for a quiet life. If he had misgivings about Mandy he was keeping them to himself. After all, she was by far the best carer they'd had. Great references too: *We can't rate Mandy too highly ... Cheerful, efficient, hard-working ... Our mother's last months were transformed by Mandy's compassion ... Mandy was our Angel.*

Maybe it was she herself who was sarky. Had she thought of that? Maybe somewhere, lurking deep down, there was a nasty little worm of resentment – even, God forbid, jealousy – that Mandy had planted herself in the centre of their father's affections. Mandy, the cuckoo in the nest, nudging the real children out with her great buttocks, the way she'd nudged Phoebe in the kitchen.

What a ludicrous image! Phoebe blushed. Despite Robert's

accusation she was no drama queen. She just had a vivid imagination. After all, she was an artist.

This reminded her of something else Mandy said, something that needled her. It was during lunch and she was describing her tumbler paintings, the cow parsley ones.

'What happens when you put them in the dishwasher?' Mandy asked.

'You can't do that.'

'You've got to wash them up by hand?'

'You can't wash them up at all.'

'Pardon?'

'They're not to be *used*.'

Mandy looked at her. 'You mean you can't drink from them?'

'No.'

'Not at all?'

'No.'

She paused. 'Oh.'

'They're art objects,' Phoebe said irritably. 'Collectors' items.'

She didn't know why she felt rattled. There was something about that pale, doughy face, challenging her in some indefinable way. The woman knew nothing about art, she didn't have a clue. Her father just smiled his vague smile.

Phoebe pulled out her easel. But she couldn't concentrate. She gazed across the yard, at the back of the butcher's shop. At the boy, Karl, who was skinning a rabbit, peeling it like a glove. *Gone to fetch a rabbit skin, to wrap the baby Bunting in.*

Robert

Robert was watching his wife through the window. They were at a party in Notting Hill and he was skulking in the garden. Farida, as usual, was at the centre of an adoring huddle. Moths, flames. She wore her yellow silk dress. Robert was loitering behind one of those obligatory olive trees in its obligatory terracotta pot. There were eight of the bastards, bloody enormous, shipped from Tuscany, no doubt, like Birnam Wood to Dunsinane. His host was a newspaper magnate who had addressed him as Richard before swinging round to shake the hand of a Tory minister.

In the old days Robert could smoke. His excuse, now, was the mobile clamped to his ear. He tilted his head attentively, listening to its non-existent messages. God, he hated these parties. Farida used to catch his eye through the crowd but those days were long gone. *I don't do dote.* Others did, however. She was beautiful and brainy and famous. Funny, too, unless you happened to be at the sharp end. He was used to being ignored, watching the crowd around her roaring with laughter while he was stuck with the host's personal trainer. Or their accountant. Or even, on one occasion, the mother of the caterer, who had been called in to help with the washing-up.

Actually this had always happened, even in the old days

when he was, ostensibly, Somebody. Mentioning that he worked in the City would result in a flickering of the eyes round the room and a disappearance in search of a refill. Farida would be the magnet, Farida the reason they had been invited in the first place.

In the early years Robert didn't mind. He was proud of her. But as nobody spoke to him he felt he had less and less to say. Even, weirdly, to himself. His lack of confidence, Phoebe would say, stemmed from their childhood. Absent father, resentful mother who found it difficult to show affection, that sort of thing. No doubt his sister explored this in her various therapy groups. The last he heard it was qigong, whatever that was. Knockton was full of that sort of nonsense.

A man burst out of the house, bellowing into his mobile, and strode around the garden. 'Where's my fucking jacket?' he yelled. From what Robert could tell, coffee had been spilled on it during a flight from LA and the airline seemed to have lost it.

Robert took no notice, standing there with an attentive expression, the dead phone to his ear.

And then it actually rang. He jumped.

'Dad?'

It was Alice, his daughter.

'Where are you?' she asked.

He told her whose party it was but she hadn't heard of them. 'The PM's right-hand chap is here too, apparently,' he said. 'Someone saw him coming out of the bog.'

Alice wasn't interested in that either. She knew nothing about current affairs, despite her mother's job. Nothing about his and Farida's world. In fact, he could hardly remember her reading a book. She was sporty, that was why. Never happier than when running some marathon and sucking protein drinks from those strangely infantile plastic bottles, the ones with the teats. He loved her, of course, but sometimes she didn't seem like his child at all.

'I wanted to try out this new bike,' Alice was saying. 'The one I told you about, the Fuji SL. So yesterday I took it on the train to Charlbury, to get off there and ride it to Cheltenham. That was my plan, it was such a lovely day. So I was just riding through Burford when I thought – *duh*, why don't I drop in on Granddad? I tried to phone but I couldn't get a signal, so just pitched up there.'

'How was he?'

'Fine. They were watching some game show. I was bursting so I ran upstairs to the bathroom – I didn't go to the downstairs loo because you can hear everything. Anyway, so I ran upstairs and Granddad's door was ajar – the door to his old bedroom. And I saw this funny thing—'

'*Robert!*'

He swung round. Farida stood there, breathing heavily.

'What are you *doing*?' She glared at him. 'It's so *rude*.'

'I'm talking to our daughter.'

'You've been out here for *ages*.'

'I'll come in a sec.'

She gave him one of her looks, turned and went back into the house, her heels clacking on the flagstones.

'What funny thing?' he asked Alice.

'His desk drawers were open, and there were some papers spread out on the floor – papers and photographs.'

'What papers?'

'I don't know, I didn't go in, I was dying for a crap. And

when I came out of the bathroom the door was closed.' She paused. 'I mean, he can't get upstairs any more, can he?'

'No.'

'I didn't say anything because it didn't strike me at the time. I'd forgotten he couldn't get upstairs. I just thought about it later, when I was biking along. That it was a bit funny. And the door being open when I went in and closed when I came out. That was a bit odd too.'

Maybe he should have told Phoebe. The trouble was, his sister was so nervy. She'd already expressed unease about Mandy and he didn't want to spook her. And there was probably a perfectly rational explanation. Dad had asked Mandy to search for something in his desk, what was wrong with that? And she'd hurried upstairs to close the door . . .

Now why would she do *that*?

He decided to put it out of his mind. He needed every ounce of concentration for his novel. It was now thickly peppered with dialect words. Whole phrases, too. He'd emailed another list to his sister, who had given it to Torren. He was no longer her fuckbuddy – the fellow deserved more respect than that – he was *Torren* now. Though he'd never set eyes on the chap, Robert felt a bond with him, not just because of his help, invaluable though that was. No, it was a stronger, more intimate connection, woven deeply into the characters he had brought so thrillingly to life. And the book was rattling along. By mid-April Robert had written 10,000 words. This was enough, he reckoned, to be submitted to a publisher, with a synopsis of the rest.

He already had an agent, of sorts. This was an amiable old soak called Barnaby Rivers, one of the last of the legendary Soho hell-raisers and now in his dotage. Robert had met him in Knockton some years earlier, when he was visiting his sister. Barnaby was an old drinking buddy of the chap who ran the hotel there. He should have been put out to grass years ago, but he kept on a few clients for old times' sake. Robert suspected that he had taken him on, a new author, due to his rural theme; some novel set in the wilds of Lincolnshire had just been shortlisted for the Booker.

Robert pressed *send* and leaned back in his chair, fingers laced behind his head. Needless to say, he felt a profound sense of satisfaction. In the garden a host of golden daffodils were fluttering and dancing in the breeze. Roll over, Wordsworth! Make way for one more!

To be perfectly honest, he couldn't actually picture his characters' faces. They existed in a sort of blur. What he could picture, however, was Farida's expression when his novel was accepted. On her lovely features was a look of surprise – yes, he would expect that. But there would also be something he hadn't seen for years – well, not directed at himself, anyway. A look of admiration and respect. Even, just maybe, *awe*. That would be a new one.

Robert was still vaguely puzzled, however, by what Alice had said and decided to ask his father about it on his next visit. Trouble was, he couldn't get him alone. Mandy fussed around him, or remained within earshot. 'Your father's a little out of sorts,' she said, 'aren't you, Jimmy?'

One of the reasons was the start of the tourist invasion. It was the Easter holidays and the lane outside was jammed with coaches, their engines idling. His dad, when shuffling past on the way to the donkeys, had thwacked one of the coaches with his stick and had woken the slumbering driver who had told him to fuck off.

World events were also getting him down. A lifelong leftie, he was horrified by the rise of right-wing xenophobia and intolerance all over Europe. He couldn't discuss this with Mandy, of course. She'd already made plain her opinion about foreigners.

'I miss your mother,' he said to Robert, his eyes filling with tears. 'Spring is so cruel.'

His wife's daffodils were coming up in the flowerbeds – always later than London. She had loved this garden, though now it looked sadly neglected. During their retirement years she had transformed it, lugging back loads of plants and damp, leaden, Swiss rolls of turf from the local nursery. As he'd once observed: 'A gardener's handiest tool is his wallet.'

He missed his wife humming to herself as she dug and watered, wearing her ancient denim dungarees, her grey hair escaping from its scarf. Never one for exercise, he had sat in the love-seat they had bought for their golden wedding anniversary, reading the newspaper to her as she toiled.

But most of all he missed the conversation. The two of them talked non-stop – about politics, books, big things. They were intellectual soulmates, and though they often quarrelled it never descended into the needling personal attacks, the chronic war of attrition and occasional eruptions of resentful venom with which Robert was only too familiar. It was about things that mattered. His mother was highly intelligent and he knew she was frustrated but she loved her husband dearly and theirs really was a marriage of true minds. Maybe it was a generational thing, a certain acceptance and compromise that was now more or less extinct. Or maybe they were just lucky.

On this visit Robert failed to get his father alone. Mandy was always around. She seemed watchful – in fact, downright tense. This was unlike her. The old man told a rambling story about a conference in Prague and she caught Robert's eye as if to say, *He's losing the plot.* He had, indeed, already complained twice about a crowd of paparazzi who had descended on the local shop when some celebrity was visiting, but that didn't seem too worrying. According to Robert's family he, too, was always repeating himself.

Besides, it gave him the chance to broach the subject.

'Talking about photos,' he turned to Dad, 'I was wondering if you've got that one of Jack and his first car. He wants to show it to his girlfriend.'

'Probably,' he replied. 'It'll be in my desk, bottom drawer.'

There was a moment's silence. Then Mandy said: 'I saw some photos the other day, now you mention it.' She turned to his father. 'Remember, love, you asked me to go through some papers for you.'

He looked confused. 'Did I?'

'Yes, pet.'

'What papers?'

'Some old bills,' she said. 'Council Tax bills.'

'Why?' he asked.

'Don't you remember?' She massaged his cuticles. 'They'd

been putting you in the wrong band, but I rang them and sorted it out. Don't worry.'

He still seemed confused. She gave Robert a significant look. *See what I mean?*

A cascade of song came from the kitchen. Three o'clock: the blackbird.

'Time for your nap,' said Mandy.

His father didn't move. He was gazing at the garden, now blurred by rain. 'It's funny,' he mused. 'I can remember the past so clearly. Every inch of the garden in Hampstead, when I was a child. The damp moss around the water butt, the smell of the privet in the shrubbery where I used to hide. So vivid, even though it was nearly eighty years ago. And yet, what happened last week . . .' His voice trailed away as he gazed at his legs. Nowadays he wore tracksuit bottoms. Mandy said this was more comfortable as he spent most of the day in his armchair, but they made him look as if he had relinquished hope. 'People say about childbirth, nobody could describe it, and if they did, nobody could bear to go through with it.' He raised his head and looked at them, his eyes moist. 'None of us know about *that*, of course. Childbirth. But I do know about *this*, and you can take my word for it. The same applies.'

'I think Mandy's been snooping around,' Robert told his sister. 'There was a funny look in her eye.'

'What sort of look?'

'Just . . . funny. I mean, it seemed perfectly plausible that Dad had forgotten. He's forgetting a lot of things nowadays. But then I went upstairs to the loo, and checked in his desk. He doesn't have bills in there, nothing like that.

It's photos and letters and personal stuff – marriage certificates, his will, our old school reports. The bills and Council Tax demands are in his filing cabinet on the landing.'

There was a silence the other end. Then she said: 'Doesn't sound that suspicious to me.'

'Really?'

'She could have been looking in his desk and not found it, whatever it was. The Council Tax thing.'

Her reaction surprised him. He hadn't expected her to be so unconcerned. After all, *she* had been the one who'd first voiced doubts about the woman.

'Maybe next time you visit you could keep your eyes open, watch out for anything odd,' Robert said. 'When *are* you going down, by the way?'

'Not for a couple of weeks,' she said. 'I'm awfully busy.'

Ah, Robert thought. She doesn't want to be bothered. Everything's fine, don't poke around. Imagine the kerfuffle of trying to find somebody new. One of them would have to uproot their lives and move in with their father, miles away in that mausoleum of a village, shopping and cooking and taking care of him. Then they would have to start that whole exhausting process all over again – interviews, references, trial runs, disappointments and sackings. It could take weeks. Months.

Robert realised, as he put the phone down, that Phoebe had reacted in just the way she'd accused *him* of reacting on that earlier occasion. *Better the devil you know.*

Though *devil* seemed an inappropriate way of describing their dumpy little godsend – Mandy from Solihull, with her bobble hat and cheery laugh – Mandy, without whom their lives would fall apart. More like an angel, in fact, than a devil.

Phoebe

Of course Phoebe was busy. She'd decided to have another go at internet dating. She hadn't done it for a couple of years but she'd been encouraged by Angie, who ran the eponymous Angie's Bistro in the High Street. Like Phoebe, Angie was no spring chicken. Terrific bone-structure, though, and masses of blond hair, which she piled up on top of her head and fixed with a plastic gardenia. Hungry mouth, tanned and wrinkled cleavage. She was the widow of a famous rock 'n' roll guitarist and had brought some much-needed glamour into their community of beardies and herbalists. Phoebe suspect the bistro was just a hobby.

Angie had recently started an affair with a man she'd met online and said Phoebe should have another bash, darling. Phoebe had bumped into her in Costcutter. 'He's dynamite in the sack,' she said, 'despite the gammy leg. And I don't want to die alone, being eaten by rats.' The queue was silenced by this. Even the cashier paused to listen.

Phoebe couldn't imagine Torren at her deathbed, so she took her advice and logged onto Soulmates. Perhaps unwisely she'd been honest about her age and the only response she'd got so far was a man called Arnold who lived in Leominster. He said he liked golf but Phoebe didn't hold that against him, remembering Bob Dylan did too.

And Obama. Arnold's wife had died and he lived in a bungalow with two Alsatians.

As she drove there Phoebe thought about her parents' marriage. Sixty-four years they had been together. Sixty-four years of rock-solid adoration since meeting at Oxford. Never wavering, never straying, an ever-fixed mark that looks on tempests and is never shaken.

And there was she, with a trail of disastrous relationships behind her and still flailing around, still out there in the jungle – literally so, in the case of Torren. There was no way she could compete; she had long ago given up trying. For she had realised that both she and Robert were casualties of their parents' devotion and had spent their lives trying to provoke a reaction.

She herself had gone the traditional route – drugs, sex, the usual teenage stuff. A brief marriage to an alcoholic who'd turned out to be a serial philanderer. Various entanglements with men so unsuitable that even her mild and tolerant father, much to her gratification, had voiced his concern. *They're not good enough for you, darling.* She was a free spirit, a rebel! Indeed, she sometimes snorted the odd line with Torren, just to show she could still do it. What on earth was she trying to prove?

Her brother had taken another route. The brash, willy-waving City route. It really wasn't his thing at all. No wonder he came a cropper. But she knew why he did it. He wanted to be a real man. He wanted their dad to be startled into some kind of respect. Their dear, left-wing Dad, safe in the arms of academia, had no idea of the testosterone-driven insanity of the trading floor. Nor, as it turned out, had Robert.

And now their father was an enfeebled old man who had become an enthusiastic reader of the *Daily Mail,* surely a sign of senility. Their mother was dead. They didn't have to prove themselves any more. Which seemed to make no difference at all.

Arnold had suggested they meet at Starbucks in the High Street. When she saw him Phoebe's heart sank. She was faced with a shrivelled old gnome, barely recognisable from his photo. This plummeting sensation, familiar for anyone engaged in internet dating, worsens with age, for she was slap up against the mirror of her own mortality. She was *that* old? He could barely struggle to his feet to shake her hand.

I don't want to die alone, being eaten by rats. We all need to be cared for at the end of our lives. More often than not, this person will be a stranger. When Rejoice from Zimbabwe was living with him, her father whispered: 'A black face sees us into this world and a black face will see us out.' Phoebe was startled at the time but she understood what he meant.

Arnold, like her father, needed a carer. He had only recently been widowed. When Phoebe helped him home with his shopping there was still a box of his wife's incontinence pads in the hallway. He was utterly helpless and the Alsatians couldn't cook his dinner so he had wasted no time in trying to find somebody as a replacement. He practically asked her, *When can you start?* before she made her excuses and left.

This encounter was curiously upsetting. Phoebe thought: I should be with my dad. Suddenly, she missed him so sharply it took away her breath. How could she leave him to a professional when she was his *child?* Leominster was on the way to the Cotswolds; it would only take an hour to drive to his house.

When she phoned the landline, however, there was no answer. She rang Mandy's mobile.

'We're on one of our jaunts, aren't we, Jimmy?' Mandy said.

'Where are you?'

'We're having a smoothie in Kenilworth,' she said. 'At the Hedgehog Rescue Centre. They're ever so nice, the people who run it, and they've all come out of hibernation now.'

Phoebe's father said something and Mandy burst out laughing.

'I mean the hedgehogs!' she spluttered. 'Silly me!'

They murmured together again. Phoebe heard her father's chuckles. For a moment, ridiculously, she felt excluded.

Her father came on the line. 'We've been having a lovely day,' he said. 'Mandy has such marvellous ideas. This place is a real tonic. There's good in the world, you see. The way they care for these little creatures, some of them arrive in a terrible state. Janice and Don, the owners, they're filled with such love and compassion. They're carers, you see, just like our Mandy here.'

Tears suddenly filled Phoebe's eyes – fierce, jealous tears. 'I'm longing to see you,' she said. 'Shall I come next Saturday?'

'Of course! We're not doing anything, are we, Mandy?'

*

On Friday, however, Torren phoned. Phoebe was watching her sister-in-law on the breakfast news, the morning's atrocities pouring from her lips. She was pleased to see that Farida was wearing a turquoise pendant she'd given her at Christmas.

'You free on Saturday?' Torren asked. 'Want to come to a motorbike show at Stafford?'

Phoebe was stunned. He'd never asked her out, ever.

He explained that he needed a part for his bike, and his van was on the blink. In other words, would Phoebe give him a lift? She was still flattered, her stupid heart thumping as she put down the phone.

So she cancelled her father and found herself in a damp field somewhere in the Midlands looking at boxes of rusting motorbike entrails. Exhausts, sprockets, pistons.

Torren's bike was apparently a BSA A65. 'The carburettors need re-jetting,' he said. 'The float chambers are gunged up something chronic.'

He rummaged in the boxes. Leaning against him, Phoebe felt a sexual throb. She was his date, his biker chick. Ageing, but so what? There were plenty of equally raddled females there with their grizzled old Hell's Angels, several of whom were in wheelchairs and, in one case, minus a leg. Torren himself was apparently the survivor of several legendary smashes. 'Had a Yamaha XS-2, went like fuck but the handling was rubbish on corners.'

They squelched across the grass to look at rows of motorbikes. Men squatted on their haunches, inspecting and prodding them as if they were livestock. Torren started talking to a group of them and, as it had started to rain, Phoebe told him she would wait for him in the café.

It was in a vast hangar filled with stalls of leather clothing and biking paraphernalia. Phoebe sat down with a mug of tea and tried to phone her father but there was no signal. Actually he hadn't sounded too upset when she'd cancelled her visit. Besides, it was Robert's turn. Apparently he'd sent off his novel – some chapters and a synopsis – so he no longer had an excuse to stay away, pretending to be busy.

Phoebe imagined him on tenterhooks, waiting for a response. Of course she hoped his book would be published. He'd been working on it for years, and it would restore his beleaguered self-respect. Even his children, nowadays, treated him with vaguely amiable contempt. His novel sounded pretty turgid to her but some people might like that sort of thing – rapes and castrations and lots of mud. According to Robert, the Radnorshire vocabulary had transformed it into something blisteringly real, and he had Torren to thank for that. No longer did he sneer at him for being her bit of rough. Torren was now that rarest of creatures: a genuine local with his roots deep in the vernacular.

There was no sign of him, however, and Phoebe realised that an hour had passed. It was getting late and the crowd was thinning. People were starting to pack up their stalls and behind her the café shutter came down with a clatter.

She got up and went outside. The rain was heavy now and most people had gone. A few remaining bikes were being wheeled away and in the next field the car park was emptying.

She went indoors and searched the hangar. She waited beside the gents, in case Torren was in there. She tried his phone but of course there was no signal.

After a while she realised he had gone.

*

'You *forgot* all *about* me?'

'I'm sorry, doll.'

'You forgot all about me and just went *home*?'

'Yeah.'

It was the next morning and Torren had arrived at her house to apologise. Apparently he'd seen a mate of his who used to run the Wall of Death. It was raining so hard that they'd retreated to his van where they'd smoked some weed. Torren had lost all track of time – and, apparently, any memory of herself. The guy had offered him a lift home and he'd taken it.

'I can't *believe* it,' Phoebe said.

'I realised halfway back and I tried to phone you but I couldn't get a signal.'

'Do I really mean so little to you?'

'That's so not true, sweetheart.' He rummaged in a plastic bag and gave her a bunch of daffodils. He'd probably picked them on the bypass.

'It does make me feel just a tiny bit used.'

Torren sat down at the kitchen table. It was odd seeing him in her house, the church bells ringing the faithful to prayer and him slumped there scratching his wiry grey rats'-tails.

'You mean a hell of a lot to me,' he said.

'I don't think so.'

'You do. Straight up.'

'Oh, yes?' She shoved the daffodils into a jug. 'Me, and how many others?'

Phoebe regretted this the moment she said it. He gazed at her, his eyes periwinkle-blue in that narrow, weathered face. 'Shall I tell you a secret? My heart goes pitter-patter when I see your little yellow car come down the lane. I feel like I'm young again. I know that's stupid, but it's true. There's nobody else does that to me. So put that in your pipe and smoke it, Miss Wentworth.'

There was a silence. The bells had stopped and all she could hear was her beating heart. Torren had never spoken like this before. Their little fracas had shunted them into an unexpected intimacy and for this she was grateful.

The atmosphere relaxed. Phoebe made some coffee. Torren wandered around the kitchen picking up things and putting them down again. She felt absurdly touched by his bashful demeanour and battered daffodils. He'd never given her a gift before, though sometimes his dog dropped dead animals at her feet. They had a proper conversation about the proposed supermarket and what it might do to the town, which he seemed as fond of as she was.

'When I was a boy,' he said, 'my dad used to drive his sheep to market here every week. He sat in his tractor herding them down the hills and into the High Street. It was fucking slow – should've seen the traffic jam. Then, when he'd sold 'em, we'd stock up on supplies and drive back to the farm.'

When he'd finished his coffee he kissed Phoebe on the cheek and left. This chaste goodbye, for some reason, moved her more than anything. In fact, on that Sunday morning she felt herself becoming close, very close, to falling in love with him.

Robert

Robert woke up feeling weightless – a floating nonentity, filled with dread. The taste of abandonment soured his mouth. In his dream he'd been a baby again, alone in his pram, in some vast supermarket whose aisles stretched into infinity. His mother was nowhere to be seen, and he knew he had lost her for good.

He kicked aside the duvet and lay there, drenched in sweat. The house felt echoing, with his last child gone. It had been three years since Alice had moved out but he could still feel her absence dizzyingly, like vertigo.

Farida lay on the far side of the bed; it was her day off. She was curled up, the duvet heaped on top of her. Was she asleep or was she faking it? She looked as artfully arranged as an actress in a movie – the tousled hair, the glimpse of silk strap against the burnished mahogany of her shoulder. Just for a moment he couldn't quite believe in her, that she belonged to him or truly lived in this house. This large, immaculate house that had so briefly held his children before they disappeared. He felt a throb of homesickness for the terrace down the road where they had been as snug as puppies. The marks on the walls to celebrate their children growing. The scuffs and scars of family life.

The sun glowed through the blinds. It was late, nearly nine o'clock, but Robert couldn't move. He had a powerful feeling that he was alone, inching towards death, each passing hour a chirrup of birdsong from his father's mad clock a hundred miles away. Actually, come to think of it, no madder than anything else.

His dream had been triggered by something Phoebe told him. Apparently Torren had abandoned her at a motorbike show in Staffordshire. 'As if I didn't exist,' she said.

She'd made it into a joke but his heart had ached for her. Why did she always choose such hopeless men? Was her self-esteem so low that chaps like Torren were all that she deserved?

Robert knew the answer, of course. Since their mother died they'd been talking a lot about their childhood. Her death had peeled open the lid of the past, raw and exposed. So had their dad's transformation into a doddery old man, alone and therefore vulnerable to their examination of his fatherly shortcomings. Their conversations about this, during the past four years, had eased the old rivalry between them.

Dear Phoebe. Only his darling, neurotic sister truly understood him. Free-floating anxiety, existential angst, bottomless sense of failure – this was meat and drink to her. Farida had no patience with this sort of talk and some-how transformed it into an attack on him. *You would say that. Huh, typical! Why do you always go on about how YOU feel?* Anything could be used as an excuse to get at him. Take his dad. *Huh. Catch us farming our father out. You English are very odd.*

Robert *was* feeling odd – weird and untethered, like a helium balloon slipping from his own fingers and floating helplessly away. This was partly to do with his novel. It had now been sent to a publisher and his sense of loss was as

profound as when his children left home. Not just loss –
anxiety, panic, heart-hammering fear. What was happening
to it, at this moment? Was somebody thumbing through its
pages and sneering at his bumbling attempt at a story? Did
they believe in any of it? He missed its company, and his
treks during the winter to his shed. He even missed the
wicker chair that gave him backache, and its reeking, mil-
dewed cushion.

Barnaby, his agent, had liked it but then he was easy to
please. 'Splendid, dear boy!' he'd said on the phone. 'I'll
whack it off to Ellie Hill at Aintree Books, it's right up her
Strasse.' A glass clinked.

Now this Ellie Hill held his life in her hands and he
hadn't heard anything for two weeks. What was she doing
now? Reading his book or carousing with her friends in
some artisanal alehouse? Washing her tights, his manuscript languishing under a pile of its rivals? Robert
examined her photo on the Aintree Books website. Young,
of course; they were all pre-schoolers. She looked unnerv-
ingly glossy and metropolitan. Would she understand the
travails of a Radnorshire farming community a hundred
years ago? Did *he* understand it? Had he truly got to grips
with it at all? Would Aled and Cadog and that poor, abused
Llinos – names he'd found on Google – come alive for
young Ellie Hill from Bounds Green or Lewisham or wher-
ever ambitious young editors could afford to live in London
nowadays? He was already resenting her for taking so long,
yet mentally smarming up to her in case she was reading it
at this moment. It was agony.

He left Farida to her lie-in and went downstairs to make
breakfast. As he ground the coffee beans his mobile rang.

It was Mandy.

'Everything's hunky-dory,' she said. 'But your dad's wondering if you're coming today. He has it in his diary but, well, you know what he's like.'

Christ, he'd forgotten all about it.

It was the most beautiful day – sun shining, blue sky. If April is the cruellest month, May is the peacemaker. Wisteria smothered the porches of the embalmed cottages. A huddle of tourists stood outside the shop, shaking out a map. Somewhere a dog barked – wearily, repetitively, as if a log was being sawed. It was a Tuesday and nothing much was happening, but then nothing ever did. For eight years his parents had lived in Chipping Norbury and Robert had no idea how they passed the time until his mother's death had swooped Dad's life into close-up. He was still feeling weightless, and this bland picture-postcard beauty felt as unreal as Farida posing in bed a few hours earlier, pretending to be asleep, pretending to be his wife.

He seemed no longer to be able to make connections. Long ago Chipping Norbury had been knee-deep in blood and guts. People had struggled for existence, scraping a living in howling gales; farmers like Llinos, Aled and Cadog, who had seemed so real in his shed. Now, in this village of manicured lawns, he simply couldn't believe in them at all. Had people like that really lived here? Lived anywhere? His characters seemed costumed mannequins, wound up like clockwork. He had a horrible feeling that Ellie Hill, whoever she was, had sussed him out. That accounted for her silence.

As he parked the car Robert remembered something

Phoebe had told him. They were talking more nowadays; Phoebe's life, like their father's, was coming into sharper focus. Apparently she sang in some sort of choir. It consisted of people like her – ageing hippies with impeccable *Guardian* credentials, mostly women, of course. Every Wednesday they performed for the old people in the East Radnorshire Day Centre.

'We've been trying to open their minds to other cultures,' Phoebe said. 'Some of them, would you believe, have never even gone to London. Certainly never seen a black face.'

So the choir had learned the words of a Tutsi creation anthem. A lot of warbling and clicking, apparently, it had taken them weeks to master it. The old dears, most of whom suffered from dementia, had gamely sung along.

'It was only afterwards,' said Phoebe, 'that we discovered it was a lament for a stillborn son.'

Robert had laughed at the time, but now he thought that nothing is quite as it seems. We think we know the words, but reality can be brutally different.

Something he was going to find out, in the weeks ahead.

'He hasn't been too well,' said Mandy. 'He's had a urinary infection.'

'Why didn't you tell me?'

'That's why he might seem a little confused. The kidneys can have that effect with older patients. I've seen it before. But it's fine. We went to the doctor and he's been prescribed ciprofloxacin. He's much better today, aren't we, Jimmy?'

His father did look disorientated, his white hair as fluffy as a baby bird's. His puzzle book lay open on his knee. 'When are we going to the donkeys?' he asked.

'Later,' she said. 'Your son's here now.'

'I know he's here! He's standing in front of me, I'm not completely ga-ga. I just thought it's a nice little walk and the hawthorn blossom's lovely. One of England's unsung glories, and it might be the last year I'll see it.'

'Dad!'

'I'm a scientist, my boy. I've spent my life facing the facts.' With his finger, he traced the scalloped lace of the antimacassar. 'Dispassion can be a comfort, you know. As Daniel Dennett, the great American rationalist, said, "Not a single one of the cells that compose your body knows who you are or cares."'

'Stop it!' Mandy shivered. 'You're giving me goose bumps.'

'I find it strangely invigorating,' he said.

Mandy took off her specs and polished them on her cardigan. 'What those cells need is a nice cup of tea. And if we're *very* good, we can have a caramel custard.'

She gave Robert a wink and put on her specs. *Stop infantilising him!* he wanted to shout, as she heaved herself to her feet.

He thought: old age is the loneliest place on earth. Not only do you lose your dearly beloved. You lose, one by one, the people whose shared memories fill your head. Stealthily, as they fade to black, their voices are silenced; nothing and nobody can fill that gap. Nobody else will *get it* like that person did. Nobody is left who knew you when you were young.

He listened to Mandy clattering about in the kitchen. And then you end up living with somebody who doesn't get the joke, who's not your type. Who you have nothing in common with apart from your survival. Stuck with each other day and night like a terrible arranged marriage. Surely this is the loneliest thing of all.

His father had sunk into himself that day, and who could blame him? Robert gazed at a list his dad had written, pinned to the wall: 'NEBULOUS. HOSIERY. LUXEMBOURG.' Words peripheral to his life that he nevertheless didn't want to lose.

Robert needed to talk but Dad seemed querulous and detached. 'Any news about your book?' he asked, but when Robert told him about the editor, Ellie Hill, his gaze wandered around the room, as if these surroundings were new to him and vaguely surprising. *How have I fetched up here? Where's my Anna?*

Robert shouldn't have felt deflated. One has to make allowances, with the elderly. But he didn't want to. He wanted his old father back, bristling with questions. He didn't want to treat his dad like an invalid.

Ah, but had he ever been that interested? Really interested? He was a scientist, through and through. When Robert brought him a toad his dad told him about its life cycle but he'd never asked him how he felt when his first girlfriend, Alison Sykes, dumped him. It was his mother who had laid her hand on his shoulder and said, 'You poor boy, this is just the beginning.' Though how she knew about it, with her happy marriage, God knew.

Robert and his father relapsed into silence. It was almost a relief when Mandy came in with the tea tray. As she passed around the biscuits she talked about her new best friend, Bianka, from Hungary, who worked at the pub.

'She's not a scrounger, not like those others. Before she came here she worked at Spearmint Rhinos, sitting on men's knees. She didn't like that so then she worked cleaning toilets.'

'She's got a BA in Oceanography,' said his dad. 'A surprising choice for a lass from a landlocked country.'

As the two of them discussed Bianka, his father perked up. The conversation moved on to Bianka's ne'er-do-well boyfriend, who worked in the carwash at the Banbury Sainsbury's.

'Bianka's found out he's having an affair with one of the mums who shops there,' said James eagerly. 'But she's too weak to leave him. She says that when he's with her, she's putty in his hands. She says he *gets* her, if you know what I mean, and there's simply no arguing with that, though we've tried our best, haven't we, Mandy?'

To be frank, this exchange irritated Robert. Here he was, his father, talking about feelings all of a sudden – not something that had engaged him much in the past. And he seemed far more interested in what Mandy was telling him than anything Robert said.

Robert knew this was petty. *This* was his dad's universe now: his carer, the small goings-on in his small village. But still it rankled. Once or twice, during tea, Robert caught Mandy giving him a speculating look. Did she guess what was going on in his head?

He still hadn't quite worked her out – whether she considered herself an employee or whether *they* were the ones who were beholden to her. He and his sister. Whether she respected them for what they were doing, or whether she despised them for not having proper jobs.

Huh! Robert thought. Just wait till my novel's published. See your face then!

'What's the joke?' Mandy was looking at him.

'Nothing.'

They were interrupted by a chirrup from the kitchen.

'Aha, the chiff-chaff!' said his dad.

'No, love, the warbler. Four o'clock.'

'Silly me.' His dad dunked his biscuit in his tea. 'We're going on a jaunt tomorrow.'

'Only if your temperature's back to normal,' said Mandy.

'We're going to visit her flat in Droitwich.'

'What flat in Droitwich?' Robert asked.

'Her flat.' He pointed to Mandy. 'One of her old boys left it to her.'

'What do you mean?'

'In his will.'

Robert turned to Mandy. 'Wow. That was generous.'

She shrugged. 'The tenants are leaving and I want to check it over.'

Robert sat there, astonished. Dad and Mandy drank their tea.

'We're looking forward to it, aren't we, dear?' said Mandy. 'We're going to have lunch at Pizza Express.'

He felt a sinking sensation in his bowels. A *flat*? She'd been left a *flat*?

He phoned his sister the next morning.

'That's what she was doing that day,' he said. 'She was looking at his will.'

'Why?'

'To see if he'd changed it in her favour. Maybe to *change* it in her favour. Fake his signature, something like that. Maybe she did that with the old man who left her the flat.'

'Don't come all novelistic with me,' said Phoebe. 'Save it for your work.'

Robert was walking on Wimbledon Common. The sun shone, birds were singing their little hearts out. Pedigree dogs crashed through the undergrowth, followed by trophy wives who, like him, were shouting into their mobiles. Happiness swept through him – a gust of it, like a freak wind. He was in this lovely wood on a Wednesday morning, as free as the invisible birds in the bushes, and would soon return to his beautiful Victorian house with its gleaming steel kitchen and four bathrooms.

Robert's unease was swept away. He would buy another dog. His novel would be published. His father was being cared for, and only a diseased mind could harbour suspicions about a woman who devoted herself to his wellbeing.

So, one of her patients had expressed his gratitude. So what? Maybe the old chap had no family and Mandy was his only friend in the world. Maybe he *had* a family but he'd been forgotten and neglected, surplus to requirements, like so many old folk.

No danger of that with Dad.

Phoebe

Phoebe was feeling guilty about her father. In the past year or so she'd only invited him over a couple of times. He didn't live far away – an hour and a half – and it wouldn't be too strenuous for him. After all, he and Mandy were always off on jaunts . . . retail parks, hedgehog sanctuaries. He'd even enjoyed visiting her mysterious flat in Droitwich. *A fun day out*, he'd said.

There was no question of him staying the night. He was beyond hotels by now, and she couldn't put him up at her place. It would just be a quick trip: lunch at the Myrtle Hotel, maybe a potter around its garden.

In fact Phoebe was sitting in the garden now, having a glass of wine with Monica and her husband, Buffy. Apparently he'd been left the hotel in someone's will – not a relative, just a friend. She would tell Robert this; surely it would allay his suspicions about Mandy. People were left things in wills, even large things like hotels and flats, when they had been good to the person in question. No doubt Mandy deserved her stroke of luck. She *was* good – kind and caring. Of course it was a paid job, looking after old people, but she went way beyond the bounds of duty.

Phoebe still considered her a godsend. She liked her more than Robert did at this point. Maybe it was a gender thing. Mandy was so clumpy and sexless, so lacking in charm. She had no idea how to flirt with a chap, the way she spoke her mind, the way she sat there with her stout legs planted apart, those tartan tights and luminous trainers. The way she stuffed herself with Battenburg cake and called their father 'Pops'. And she'd alienated Robert with her political views. It hadn't been a good start, that suggestion about his wife's job.

It was a balmy day in June. The flowerbeds looked as regimented as a municipal park's. Recently Buffy had run a residential course called Horticulture for Beginners and had got the guests to weed and re-plant his entire garden. He was a cunning sod. On his Basic Car Maintenance course he'd got them to repair his ancient Renault, and his Software for Starters guests had built him an entire website. And *they* paid *him* for the privilege.

They were talking about the proposed supermarket and its threat to their local shops. Buffy had once been an actor and had played a fishmonger in an episode of *Bergerac*.

'Had to sell John Nettles a pound of sprats,' he said. 'A pivotal moment in the plot, because I let drop the name of the murderer. I can still gut a mackerel like a professional.'

'Who were you married to at the time?' asked Monica.

He thought for a moment. 'Oh, I was vaguely with Lorna.'

'*Vaguely with Lorna?*' She glared at him. 'Didn't you have a *child* with her? Wasn't she that one?'

'I didn't know that then. We split up, you see, and she never told me she was pregnant.'

Phoebe liked Buffy. He was a big, bearded, amiable chap with a penchant for fancy waistcoats, a thespian through and through and now a gregarious hotelier. But his complicated past was a source of torment to Monica, wife number whatever. Phoebe had never quite worked it out. It was like the family tree at the beginning of *War and Peace*, which she couldn't be bothered to understand before she gave up on the book entirely.

'Wasn't she the one with the newts?' asked Monica.

'She was, bless her.'

He told Phoebe the story. Lorna lived near a wood that was going to be destroyed by a new bypass. So she'd collected some great crested newts and put them in the pond there. As they were an endangered species, the wood became designated a Site of Special Scientific Interest and the bypass was cancelled.

This struck Phoebe as deeply cunning – as cunning as Buffy's residential courses. He and this Lorna woman had a lot in common.

It was then that she had the idea.

'Isn't there a pond on the factory site?' she said. 'Where they're going to build the supermarket?'

They looked at each other. From the kitchen came the clatter of dinner preparations.

'There is,' said Monica. 'A small one, but it's definitely a pond.'

God knew where Torren found the newts. Stole them, most likely. Phoebe didn't ask. She was just glad that he was involved in this mildly lawless adventure. Their connection was thickening up into something resembling a relationship. They had even gone for a spin to Llandrindod Wells on his newly restored motorbike and had lunch in a pub like a real couple. They were having more conversations and less sex, too – again, like a real couple. In fact Torren did most of the talking but that was her fault, for asking him questions. She liked hearing about his childhood, how he ran wild over the hills from dawn to dusk, castrating lambs and rounding up stampeding bullocks, just like the characters in Robert's novel. How timid, by comparison, were their own summer holidays at Hafod!

Phoebe had decided to combine the newt transplantation with her father's visit. It would be a bit of a lark – a *hoot* – not too exhausting, and would appeal to her father's subversive nature. When they heard about it, Robert and his entire family wanted to come.

It had been months since they'd all got together. That the magnet seemed to be newts rather than Dad was something that she hoped would escape his notice.

Her father and Mandy were the first to arrive. They were accompanied by a wheelchair. 'Another *coup d'âge*,' he said, as Mandy hauled it out of the Panda.

'He's getting a bit rocky on his pins,' said Mandy. 'Aren't we, love? It's on loan from the Day Centre.'

'Wheelchair's such a depressing word,' said Dad. 'I prefer chariot.'

'We're calling her Jezebel,' said Mandy.

'She goes like the clappers,' said Dad. 'And you can hang carrier bags on her, look, and there's storage space below, and this nifty little brake. And you can go out in your bedroom slippers! Can't imagine why everyone doesn't have one.'

Each time Phoebe saw him, he seemed to have diminished. A shrunken little man, his hair thinner, his hands somehow larger. He was in good spirits, however, though his cheerful voice was at odds with a new look in his eyes. He seemed to be gazing at something in the far distance, something invisible to the rest of them. She had seen this in her mother towards the end of her life.

Don't die.

Did she say that aloud? She wasn't sure. Maybe *she* was the one who was getting dementia.

Just then Farida's huge, shiny Range Rover appeared – an essential vehicle, no doubt, in SW19. Purring down the High Street, it dwarfed the mud-spattered old bangers belonging to the locals and came to a halt outside the hotel.

'She's had the manuscript for two months!' said Robert. 'I've emailed her twice and she just said it's on her pile. Does she have no consideration?'

'She's busy,' said Farida. 'Some people do have a job, you know.'

Robert shot her a look from under his thick black eyebrows.

'I've never met anyone who's written a book,' said Mandy. 'Where do you get your ideas?'

They were having lunch at the hotel. A tartan shortbread biscuit tin sat on the table, holes drilled in its lid. Alice and Jack had squabbled like children over who should have custody of the newts and Alice – as always – had won.

'Shouldn't they have some weed with them?' she asked, lifting the lid and peering inside.

'They'll be all right for an hour or so,' Phoebe said. 'Torren knows what he's doing.'

Torren had given them the tin and disappeared; presumably he didn't want to intrude on this family gathering.

'Who was that man?' asked her father. 'Was he some kind of tramp?'

Buffy came over, carrying a wine bottle, in full Mine Host mode: paisley waistcoat, silk cravat. 'Everything OK?' he asked, indicating the food.

'Delicious,' said Farida. 'Is it locally sourced?'

'You bet,' said Buffy.

Phoebe had seen the Morrisons bags in the kitchen but she kept her mouth shut.

'If I may say, you're even more thrilling in the flesh,' Buffy said to Farida. 'The TV doesn't do you justice.'

'I did like that blouse you wore on Thursday,' said Mandy. 'We always watch the news, because it's you. We bring in our breakfast on our knees.'

'That must be awkward,' said Jack.

Mandy frowned. 'I mean, we *watch* it on our knees. I bring in our breakfast and we watch it with our trays. On our knees.'

'What's she talking about?' said Dad.

Phoebe interrupted them. 'Now, here's the plan.'

She was interested to see how Farida would react to this newt business. She was so very London. Today she wore white jeans, a cream jacket and a silky top. It was hard to imagine her squatting on her haunches beside a smelly little pond, newt in hand, in a wasteland of cracked concrete and discarded rubbish out beyond the council estate.

Just now she was talking to Mandy. They were discussing their parents. Farida, not surprisingly, had a beautiful voice. It softened when she spoke about her father and how proud she was of him. Proud of her mother, too, who had looked after the home while her father worked hard to give the children a good education, never a word of complaint, that sort of thing.

Mandy said the same. Her face glowed as she described her mother getting up before dawn to make tea for her husband before he went off on his rounds, how she devoted herself to him and her daughter. How, though money was tight, Mandy never lacked for anything, how her mother was always there for her. 'My mum used to say, *Best decision I ever made, to give up work and look after you.* Put that in your pipe and smoke it, women's libbers.'

'So was ours,' Phoebe snapped. 'Our mother was there every day, too.'

She didn't know why she found this parental love-in annoying. Was their family so dysfunctional?

She remembered it later, however; every word. The way Mandy took off her specs and polished them on her napkin, her eyes suddenly naked, and pink-rimmed with emotion.

Something unsettling happened after lunch. Mandy and Alice disappeared to the loo and after a few moments Phoebe followed them.

The Ladies consisted of two cubicles. When she arrived, both doors were closed. Mandy and Alice were in each of them, talking through the partition. She heard the stealthy trickle as they peed.

'You must have seen a lot of dead people,' said Alice.

'Some, love.'

'What's it like when they die?'

'You can tell when it's going to happen.'

'How?'

'Some of them get agitated,' said Mandy. 'Some of them

don't, it depends if they're in pain. But there's one thing that happens to all of them.'

'What's that?'

'Their feet start tingling.'

'Tingling?'

'Like, twitching and restless. Like they're getting ready for a journey.'

'Wow!'

'One of my old ladies said exactly that word.'

'What, *wow*?'

'No, *journey*,' said Mandy. ' "I'm getting ready for my journey." '

The canisters rattled as they tore off toilet paper.

'Do some of them ask to be helped on their way?'

'You mean what, exactly?' Mandy's voice was sharp.

'You know, helped to die. Like with pills or something.'

There was a silence, then the flush of a toilet. Mandy came out and bumped into Phoebe.

'Pardon.' The room was too small for someone her size. She squeezed past Phoebe, stepped to the basin and turned on the tap. Phoebe caught her eye in the mirror.

They both paused for a moment. Then Phoebe turned away.

There were five newts in the tin, nestling in damp cotton wool. Phoebe found them unexpectedly thrilling, with their dinosaur crests and orange spotted bellies. She hadn't seen a newt for years; the jolt brought back her childhood, the joy of it.

They gathered at the edge of the pond, her dad leaning forward in his chariot. Jack and Alice tenderly lifted the newts out, one by one, and placed them in the water. With a sassy little wriggle of their hips they propelled themselves into the weeds and were gone.

The little band of saboteurs were alone in the wasteland. The sun beat down on the rubble-strewn expanse of concrete. It was cracked open by buddleia bushes; Phoebe could sense, in her bones, the force of nature beneath the surface. Their branches were bowed down with cones of mauve blossoms, dancing with butterflies.

It was a moment of pure happiness. For them all; she felt it. Even Farida started laughing.

Jack and Alice wiped their hands on their jeans. 'Good work, children,' said their grandfather. 'Bugger off, Lidl. *Vive la révolution.*'

'I thought you liked Lidl,' said Phoebe.

'Not really.' He leaned back in his wheelchair and closed his eyes. Far off, in the housing estate, an ice-cream van played its tinny tune. 'If only one could choose when to die.'

'Don't, Granddad!' said Alice.

'I don't want to be a vegetable.' He turned, squinting at her in the sunshine. 'If I could choose, my darling, it would be now.'

Later, when they'd gone, Phoebe drove up to Offa's Dyke. Sitting on the grass, she watched the sunset. The hills rolled away towards the west, piled up higher and higher, mistily morphing into the clouds themselves. The sinking orange globe of the sun was companioned by a sliver of moon, waiting to take over. It knew its place, and just for this evening, so did she. Wales had drawn her back to her past and she had made it her present, here, now, amongst the harebells.

If only one could choose when to die.

Before they left, she'd taken Alice aside.

'That was a funny conversation in the loo,' she'd said. 'You and Mandy.'

'She told me how to do it.'

'Do what?'

'*It,*' said Alice. 'When we were walking back to the car. How to stockpile the morphine, even if there's a round-the-clock nurse. They watch it like a demon, apparently, but even *they* have to have a night off. There's a little pump thing and you just fill it up with a triple dose.'

'Heavens. Has Mandy done that?'

'Of course not. She wouldn't be telling me all that stuff if she'd actually *done* it, would she? She just said it was the best way to go. Peaceful. Stoned. Happy.'

Robert

Robert had always been there for his children. It was one lesson he had learned. Not for him, those broken promises. If he said he'd come to sports day, he came to sports day. Even in his high-rolling years he made sure he did, though it could be touch and go. He remembered white-knuckle taxi rides across London, sitting there drenched in sweat, the minutes ticking by.

And it had paid off. His children were a good deal less fucked-up than he and Phoebe. Yet they'd had it so much harder. For what a world they'd been bequeathed. Sky-high rents, global warming, no jobs to be found and robots taking over anyway, species wipeouts, nowhere to park.

Yet they remained optimistic, kind to their friends – much kinder, he was sure, than he was to his. Loyal, non-judgemental, thoroughly decent human beings, the world was lucky to have them. He and Farida had done at least one thing right.

Jack, a.k.a. Javed, had the advantage of his mother's good looks. Skin the colour of caramel and pale grey eyes, great bone structure, glossy black hair. Since his teenage years he'd been something of a pussy-magnet – not *his* phrase, needless to say. Robert was used to girls flirting with him, simply to get his son's attention. Jack was far too modest to consider himself a catch, which of course was part of the attraction. And he designed school playground equipment! What was not to like?

They met for lunch in a micro-brewery in Kentish Town, where Jack lived. He said how much he'd enjoyed the visit to Knockton.

The conversation turned to Mandy.

'She's well nosy, isn't she?' he said.

'What do you mean?'

'She asked me a lot of questions about you and Aunt Phoebe.'

'When?'

'When we were alone in that shop, that funny old one.'

'Audrey's.'

'Buying Granddad a vest.'

'What sort of questions?'

Jack shrugged. 'Stuff about the past, about you lot. Granny and Granddad, the family.'

'Nothing wrong with that.'

'It's just the way she did it . . . I dunno.' He pulled the crusts off his sandwich and put them on the side of his plate. He'd always done this. Then, at the end of the meal, he ate them anyway. 'Sort of casually, but sort of sharp.'

'She can be a bit abrupt.'

'Then she asked about money.'

'What?'

'She asked how you and Aunt Phoebe managed to live, when you hardly made any.'

Robert stared at him. 'I hope you told her to piss off.'

He shook his head. 'I was so surprised I just blurted out that you had, like, a private income. That's right, isn't it?'

Robert nodded.

'From some family trust thing,' Jack said. 'And anyway Mum earns lots.'

'What did Mandy say?'

' "Lucky them." ' He popped a crust in his mouth. 'Then we bought the vest.'

Robert felt a strange, queasy sensation. At the very least, it was impertinent. And why prod his son with questions? Why not ask *him*? It seemed so furtive. Then there was the mysterious rootling around amongst his father's papers, if indeed that was what Mandy had been doing.

Maybe she was just harbouring some sort of class resentment. That would be more understandable. To someone like Mandy, he and his sister led a pretty cushy life. But it still made him uncomfortable that under Mandy's cheery exterior, hostility might be lurking.

Then it was wiped from his mind, because his mobile rang. It was Barnaby, his agent.

All these weeks Robert had made up scenarios for Ellie Hill, to explain her silence. She had burned to death in a house fire and nobody had told him because his little novel was hardly a priority. Her computer had been hacked by terrorists and she'd refused to pay a ransom. She had inadvertently deleted it and was too embarrassed to tell anyone. She had gone on holiday to Costa Rica and her laptop had been stolen. She loved it so much she was reading it again, slowly, relishing every word. She had been stricken by an intestinal parasite and was laid up in hospital, blinded and unable to read. She was having a nervous breakdown. She was showing it to everyone at Aintree Books, even the canteen staff, because she thought it was so amazing she simply had to share it. She hadn't even started to read it yet.

'She's sorry she hasn't responded sooner, but she wanted to run it by her editorial director,' said Barnaby. 'They're pretty impressed. *Marvellous atmosphere,* they said, *marvellously authentic.* Congratulations, dear boy. They want to make an offer.'

Robert watched his wife on the news the next morning. He hadn't yet told her *his* news. Just for the moment, it dwarfed the ongoing carnage in the Middle East. Men ran through shattered streets clutching bundles that were only too visibly children. Horror, utter horror, yet all he could picture was Ellie Hill, his unknown angel, who was now transformed into a paragon of sensitivity and discernment.

He hadn't told Farida because they'd had a row the night before and it hadn't been the right moment. There was a sick, curdled satisfaction in this retention of his secret. Their rows were becoming more bitter and forensic; they knew each other's soft tissue so well, where it was vulnerable to the knife. And yet Robert felt he hardly knew her at all. Maybe this paradox lay at the heart of all marriages. God only knew.

Farida wanted to employ a landscape architect – someone recommended by those Notting Hill wankers with the olive trees. In fact she had gone ahead and done it.

'Why didn't you ask me first?'

'I thought you'd be all for it,' she said.

'But I like doing stuff in the garden.'

She raised her eyebrows. 'What stuff?'

'Mowing the lawn and stuff.'

'You hate mowing the lawn. You're always moaning about it.'

'I'm not.'

'If you could *hear* yourself. You've no idea how much you whinge.'

'I don't,' he said. 'Give me an example.'

'Little whinges, all the time. Like when you open the dishwasher and it's full of clean plates and you've got to empty it. You always say "fuck" under your breath. Do you know how annoying that is?'

'You do, too. A little sigh, as if *I* should have done it, I've got bugger all else to do. You make sure I bloody well hear it, too.'

She pushed back her chair and got up from the table. 'Anyway, now we don't have a dog tearing up the lawn—'

'He never tore up the lawn.'

'– I thought we could do a bit of a revamp—'

'*You* thought—'

'Maybe install a water feature—'

'*Water feature*, what a ghastly phrase.'

'– against the back wall.'

'You've been watching too many makeover shows.'

'It's just a *thought*.' She paused, a plate in each hand. 'It really would be nice if you weren't so negative. Don't you realise, you squash everything I say with a little squelch?'

'That's not true.'

'Couldn't you, for once, just be a tiny bit positive? I mean, it's not as if you'll have to *pay* for it.'

Bull's-eye. A heavy silence followed this. Farida had won. Financially, of course – she'd made *that* clear. But also morally, as she was ostentatiously clearing up dinner single-handed.

Their sulks could last for hours, sometimes for days, but this time the row flared up again and Robert slammed out of the house and walked around the block.

It was midsummer and the sky was still suffused with pink. A lone robin sang. Bitterly he pictured the water feature – some wincingly expensive marble slab, no doubt, spouting water into an arid little bowl. How different to that mucky, smelly pond in Wales, and their rare moment of joy.

They hadn't made love for three months. Farida was already in bed when he climbed in beside her. She lay with her face to the wall, pretending to sleep, but she didn't fool him.

He put his arm around her. She removed it, however, and gave it back, like a child picking up a piece of broccoli and putting it on the side of the plate.

Now, groggy from lack of sleep, Robert watched her on the breakfast news. All across Britain people were gazing at this face, as blank as a marble sculpture, with the words spilling out – ha, like a water feature! They knew nothing of the woman behind the mask. Her passive-aggression, her sulks, the constant belittling of her long-suffering husband. The way she no longer tiptoed barefoot downstairs in the mornings. The way, when she had a crap in the downstairs loo, she no longer bothered to open the window.

Mandy had broken the love-seat. The special seat in the garden, his parents' golden wedding present to each other.

'I'm ever so sorry,' she said. 'It just collapsed.'

She and James were sitting on it, she said, eating carrot cake. But Mandy was obviously the culprit. She was far too fat for its spindly legs.

Not surprisingly, his father was upset. Even more upset than Robert would have guessed. On the phone, his voice seemed close to tears.

Robert phoned Phoebe that evening and told her.

'Stupid cow,' she said. 'Have you noticed how huge she's getting? You can tell she's a binge-eater; there's something underhand about her.'

This seemed a bit harsh, but nowadays he and Phoebe see-sawed in their feelings about Mandy, and this was one of her hostile days.

'I've got an idea,' she said. 'Why don't we get Torren to make him a new one?'

She said Torren could make something special to their own design. He was a talented carpenter and he needed the work.

This seemed a good idea. After his help with Robert's book – and, to a lesser extent, the newts – the chap was owed something. Giving him a commission might be some kind of thank you.

'Though it does seem . . .' Phoebe's voice trailed away.

Robert knew what she was thinking, about their father.

'It's not a waste of money,' he said. 'He might live for years.'

Phoebe

Her father's reaction puzzled Phoebe. She thought he would be more up for it. She and Robert had emailed him some design suggestions but he didn't seem to care which one he chose, and left them to it. He usually had such good manners; now he didn't even try to make an effort.

Perhaps the loss of the seat had reminded him, with renewed force, of the loss of his wife. The times he called out, *Sun's over the yardarm,* and she downed her spade to join him for a G & T.

He once said to his daughter: 'Our marriage was one long conversation that was only interrupted by her death.' How Phoebe envied that sentence! The profound interest in each other's minds. The depth of their love – a love so deep, in fact, that her deeply rational father had come to believe in the afterlife simply because the alternative was impossible to contemplate: an Anna-shaped void in the void.

That was how Phoebe explained it to herself, at the time.

When she arrived, with the bench, James wasn't himself. Torren had borrowed a van and driven her to Chipping Norbury. The old man didn't even stir in his chair when they came into the room. He gazed at them, perplexed, as if he had no idea why they were there – indeed, just for a moment, who they were. Phoebe hadn't seen him for a few weeks and was shocked by his deterioration. His eyes looked sunken, and there was an evasive air to him that she hadn't noticed before.

Mandy lowered her voice. 'It's nothing unusual at his age, love. He's been babbling away about how much he's looking forward to seeing you and he'll talk of nothing else tomorrow. He's just away with the fairies today. It's probably the new pills.'

Phoebe and Torren carried the bench into the garden and placed it under the magnolia tree, where the other seat had been. Her father shuffled out, leaning on Mandy's arm.

'Isn't it pretty?' Mandy said. 'Have a sit-down.'

Torren had done a good job. This bench was sturdier than its predecessor, and he'd carved a swag of leaves along its back.

'Very nice,' said the old man. 'Thank you, Trevor.'

'Torren,' said Phoebe.

Her father looked around. 'The view's not the same. Has somebody cut something down?'

'Nobody's done anything,' Phoebe said. 'In fact it's getting pretty overgrown. I really ought to tidy it up a bit, while I'm here. Mow the lawn and things.'

The old man sighed. 'I miss my donkeys.'

'What's happened to them?'

'They sold the field,' said Mandy.

'What's more to the point, they'll be missing me.'

Torren sat down next to him. 'Know something? Donkeys have the longest memory of any ungulate.'

'That so?' Her father brightened. 'How on earth do they prove that?'

'Search me,' said Torren. 'You're the boffin.'

Her dad gave a grunt of laughter. They started talking about frontal lobes. Torren was well-informed; like many druggies, he was obsessed by the brain. Then, blow me down, they embarked on a discussion of astral physics.

Phoebe left them to it and went into the house to help Mandy. The kitchen window was open; from the lane she heard a tour guide, talking through a microphone to his coachload of tourists.

'He's quite a character, isn't he?' Mandy said. 'Your boyfriend.'

'My sort of boyfriend. I'm not quite sure what he is.'

'Oh, well, needs must.' She started opening a tin of pilchards. 'I haven't had time to mow the lawn, if that's what you're thinking. It's a full-time job, looking after your dad.'

'I wasn't thinking that, honestly.'

Mandy shrugged, and tipped the pilchards onto a plate. *It's all right for you, a lady of leisure.* The words hung in the air. *Dabbling away with your little paintings nobody buys.* Robert had told Phoebe about that conversation, the private income one. It really was none of the woman's business but it still made Phoebe uncomfortable.

There was an odd atmosphere that day. Her father seemed sunk into himself and hardly spoke. His eyes darted from Mandy to his daughter like a lizard waiting for a fly to land. Mandy, too, seemed watchful and uncharacteristically tense. Only Torren seemed relaxed and, in a curious way, the most at home.

So much so, in fact, that after lunch he offered to mow the lawn. Phoebe watched him trudge back and forth, leaning into the machine, his shirt flapping, his hair tied back in a rag, his back stained with a dark lozenge of sweat.

With his long spider-legs he could have been a boy of twenty; at this distance it was hard to tell. He reminded her of her past, of a long-ago holiday when she spent all night kissing some boy in a tent; a boy from the local town who she never saw again, whose name she had forgotten and who probably had grandchildren now. Who might be dead. She hadn't thought of him in forty-five years.

Siesta hour. The heat . . . the suburban drone of a lawn-mower . . . the sky criss-crossed with vapour trails. Down here on earth her father snoozed, finally grounded after a lifetime of globe-trotting. Such a big life, once.

Suddenly he opened his eyes. 'Do you remember Kunzle Cakes?' he asked. He closed his eyes again and started snoring, so loudly Phoebe thought he must be faking it.

She sat on the sofa, trying to re-spool a cassette back into its case by twirling it round with a biro, a skill that was now pretty well extinct. Her dad had some favourite audio-tapes that he refused to throw away. Opposite, Mandy was concentrating on a Sudoku puzzle, breathing heavily through her nostrils. Phoebe looked at her stumpy fingers, the nails bitten to the quick. At her soft white knees, dimpled and shockingly nude. Her summer dress was way too short, and did the woman never wash her hair?

Phoebe suddenly longed to go home, to get away from this odd, asexual woman and her unreachable father. She wanted to be in her attic bedroom with her seashells on the mantelpiece and Torren's arms around her; the view through the window of other people's gardens with their ramshackle greenhouses and small-town contentment. Today Torren seemed the only normal person here. Even leaving her at the bike show now seemed forgivable – just a typically blokey thing to do, bless him.

The window was open and she watched him mowing. He'd stripped off his shirt now to reveal his sinewy ribcage, skin kippered by the sun, and that endearing softness around his belly. Phoebe had never seen him perform such a selfless task and was suddenly flooded with love. For the first time she fantasised about them living together. She pictured a house like a child's drawing, four windows and a yellow door, with him and her inside. By now, thank God, the competition seemed to have melted away and he was spending more time with her, eating with her, rifling through her DVDs and generally making himself at home.

'He looks a bit like Iggy Pop, don't you think?' Mandy was gazing out of the window.

'Gosh, really?'

'The Iggy Pop of Croydon.'

'Croydon?'

'That's where he comes from.'

Phoebe stared at her. 'What?'

'Didn't you know?'

Robert

'Where's she taking you for lunch, this Ellie Whatsher-name?' asked Farida.

'Brasserie Zédel.'

'Hmm.' She considered this. It seemed to meet with her approval. You could never tell, with his wife.

At least it was *him* being wined and dined, for once. Perhaps, when he was a published author, people would no longer ignore him at parties. Certainly not after he'd been on *Start the Week* and had glowing reviews in the broadsheets, accompanied by a photo gazing thoughtfully out of his shed window, chin resting in hand, the classic novelist's pose.

Farida's reaction to the news had been gratifying. Her initial gobsmacked astonishment – *You must be joking!* – hadn't been too flattering but since then he had detected, lurking beneath the surface, the respect that had been missing for so long. Not *awe*, that would be pushing it, but she'd bought a bottle of champagne to celebrate and had even suggested renovating his hut as part of her garden revamp.

Robert was touched, most of all, by the way she rang up her friends to tell them the news. She wasn't by nature a boastful woman so it was a pleasure to hear her bigging him up – *he's always had a powerful imagination …*

slaving away all these years, I don't know how ANYONE can write a novel . . . I'm so proud of him.

Proud. Not a word overly used in the lexicon of their marriage. Not even when he was raking it in, during his City slicker days.

So now, freshly shaved and linen suited, he was sitting in Brasserie Zédel, a vast eatery near Piccadilly Circus, swarming with waiters and sparkling with mirrors and gilt. Opposite him sat Ellie Hill, his editor. His *editor.*

She was even younger than he had imagined. Dewy, eager, and wearing a pinafore dress that made her look like a sixth-former.

'We're all so excited!' she breathed. 'We all adore the book. Cadog and Llinos and Aled, they're all so *real*, it's such a powerful story, I mean, when they drowned the kittens I was a total basket-case.'

Barnaby, his agent, was there too, raddled and rheumy-eyed, knocking back a Scotch. In the good old days of publishing, chaps like him used to roam the plains but now they were more or less extinct.

'And it would make a marvellous TV drama,' Barnaby said. 'BBC Wales'll be gagging for it. Beautiful locations and powerful storylines, spot-on for Sunday nights.'

'I do agree,' she said. 'So thrilling. I can hardly wait for you to write the rest of it.'

'I can already see the second series,' said Barnaby.

'Would you like a *kir royale*?'

It was the moment Robert had dreamed about all these years. It still seemed like a dream; he couldn't quite connect himself up to it. He felt he was floating above the room, looking down on his moment of triumph. In the same way, his mythical Ellie still lingered, like a ghost, in her various manifestations, even with the real one sitting in front of him.

She was talking about possible delivery dates for the remainder of the novel, whether the following spring might be feasible. The *kir royale* arrived. Barnaby ordered another Scotch.

Just then Robert's mobile rang. Phoebe.

'So sorry,' he said. 'I'll have to take this. It might be about our father.'

He twisted away from them and listened to his sister's voice.

'Something awful's happened,' she said.

'What? Is it Dad?'

'It's Torren.' She paused. 'I don't know quite how to say this.'

'What?'

'I've been in floods of tears, I haven't slept a wink. I mean, it's awful for you but it's even more awful for me. I don't know what to do.'

'God, what's happened?'

'He made it all up. He's not Welsh at all. He's from Croydon.'

'*Croydon?*'

'Everything OK there?' asked Barnaby. He and Ellie were looking at him.

'He's a total fucking fraud,' hissed Phoebe. 'I feel so totally *used*.'

'I don't *believe* it.'

'Is it your father?' asked Ellie.

Phoebe lowered her voice. 'All that stuff he told you for

your book, all that Radnorshire shit, he just made it up. Those words don't exist at all.'

Apparently Torren had made up the Welsh childhood because it was more romantic. Maybe he'd started to believe in it himself. People re-invented themselves all the time, of course, especially when they came from Croydon. He said most people didn't ask about his past anyway. Most of his mates were drummers and blokes with dogs, and no doubt not over-endowed with curiosity. 'It went down well with the ladies, though,' he said. 'And it just, like, gathered its own momentum, you know?'

No. They didn't know.

Mandy found out because she recognised the Croydon accent; apparently it had its own special twang. She simply asked Torren if he came from there and his answer popped out. She'd had no idea about his fabricated past. Nor the effect of this on Phoebe.

His poor sister, so vulnerable, so insecure. So desperate for love.

She said she'd had it out with Torren on the drive home from the Cotswolds.

'And all that Radnorshire dialect?' she'd asked him. 'All those words and phrases, you just made them up?'

'Uh-huh.'

'Just like that? Off the top of your head?'

'Yeah. They just, like, came out in a rush. I was in a hurry, see, 'cos I wanted to get into your knickers.'

Robert had no idea if she was flattered by this explanation. She'd sounded utterly heartbroken to him.

'How *could* he?' she said. 'I never, ever want to see him again.'

And that day, too, his novel died.

He kept silent about this. It felt as if he'd been pregnant, and had told the world his news. Rejoicings all round. Then suddenly, after months, he'd been crippled by pain and a flood of blood and miscarried. Alone, in his shed. And it was all gone.

He knew what people would say. *Surely you could salvage it? Find out the real words, substitute them, keep calm and carry on. It's not the end of the world.*

But something mysterious had happened. His characters had lost their voice. More profoundly than that, they had lost their personalities. Their humanity. They had become utterly unknown to him and had simply faded back into the void in which they had been born. Their unwritten stories lay ahead of them but they couldn't step into them. They couldn't do anything. He hadn't a clue.

For it had all become poisoned. The falsehoods running through it had spread and made it all become tinny and untrue – what he had written and what he had planned to write. He'd totally lost his nerve.

He tried, truly he tried. He sat in his shed, laptop open. No doubt he looked like a real novelist to the Romanian gardeners now massacring the shrubbery. But all he did was noodle about on the internet.

Sooner or later he'd have to tell his family, and the publishers, and pay back his advance. But the only person he told was his sister, who was also mourning her loss.

He met her at Pret A Manger on Paddington Station. No Zédel's for those two failures.

'I feel so abused,' she said, gazing at her sandwich. 'I can't believe he could do that to me.'

She looked a wreck. At their age, tragedy could have a catastrophic effect on what remained of their looks. Phoebe was a handsome woman but her face was drained and gaunt. Once she'd been a stylish old hippie-chick but now her droopy charity-shop dress made her look like a bag lady. Her hennaed hair had frizzed into a shapeless, pubic tangle.

'I'll never get another man, not at my age.'

'Don't be daft.'

'The weird thing is, I'd pictured that farm so vividly,' she said. 'I felt I knew it, every inch. And his dad and his uncle and the bullocks. And now it's all gone. Worse than gone, poisoned. It's as if he's actually stolen my imaginary world.'

'Me, too,' Robert said. 'Join the club.'

He told her about his book, how his fictional farm had also vaporised. As he suspected, she urged him to persevere but Robert said the muse had deserted him.

'I can't paint either,' she said. 'I'm too depressed.'

'I didn't realise he meant that much to you. I thought he was just a, you know—'

'Don't!' She picked up her sandwich and put it down again. 'Actually, I was starting to care for him.'

The Tannoy announced train departures. People hurried past, pulling their wheelies behind them – people who had jobs, and loved ones to greet them.

'It's all Mandy's fault,' she said.

'*What?*'

'For blundering in and ruining everything.'

'Come on, sis. That's totally unfair.'

'Since when are things fair?'

'We'd have found out sooner or later that the chap was a fraud. In fact she's done us a favour.'

'Huh!' she snorted.

There was no arguing with her in this mood. Of course it wasn't Mandy's fault. She had just unwittingly lit the touchpaper, with no idea it would cause an explosion.

'I think she knew,' Phoebe said.

'Don't be ridiculous.'

'She's beadier than you think, digging around, snuffling around.'

'She's just interested in people, the stuff going in the village, that sort of thing.'

'She was back in Dad's room.'

His stomach sank. 'How do you know?'

'When I was there, last time. When we delivered the bench. I went upstairs to have a look and I found a biscuit wrapper in the wastepaper basket.' She took a swig of juice. 'Custard Creams.'

Robert was momentarily unnerved, he had to admit. But he tried to reassure Phoebe, as she had once reassured him. Mandy was just searching out something for their dad. She simply liked sitting there, it made a change, and it was bigger than her own room. More to the point: why on earth shouldn't she? There was no rule against it.

'Maybe it's you and me who're the nosy ones,' he said.

Besides, he had bigger things to worry about.

Phoebe

Phoebe went to the National Gallery to get her suffering into perspective. For an hour she gazed at paintings by the Italian masters. There they hung, Jesus after Jesus after Jesus. How calm he looked! And nails were drilled through his hands and feet, blood spurted from the wound in his side, he was dying a lingering death. Quite honestly, she should pull herself together.

She remembered kissing that boy in the tent all night. The lurching heart, the tender exploration. The naked skin. They were both virgins but she thought, *it can't get better than this*.

And now she was an ageing woman walking across Trafalgar Square. She looked down at her sandals; her toenails were painted blue but the varnish was chipping. No passing man would ever give her a glance, except perhaps out of curiosity, because she seemed to be crying.

Suddenly she longed for her dad. Not out of duty; just to be with him, to love and be loved. He might be a shadow of his former self but he was still her father. She could take the train to Charlbury – it was on the way home – and a taxi to his house.

But when Phoebe phoned she only got the answerphone. Ridiculously, she felt a jolt of disappointment. Why should he be there waiting for her, just because she needed him? He had a life, too.

She phoned Mandy's mobile but it was switched off.

Suddenly her self-pity vanished. What if he'd had another fall and they were in hospital? What if he'd had a stroke?

That evening, however, when she phoned again, they were home.

'I'm ever so sorry,' Mandy said. 'The mob ran out of battery. It won't happen again. I know how anxious you get.'

Was that a hidden criticism? That Phoebe was a fusspot, that her father was in safe hands?

When she asked where they'd been Mandy just said, 'Out.' She sounded distracted. 'Your dad's calling,' she said. 'I'd better toddle.'

Phoebe arranged to visit at the weekend and she rang off.

The next day Phoebe felt horribly depressed. There hadn't been a word from Torren. He'd disappeared from her life as if he'd never existed. In fact, their trysts in the wood were starting to seem more and more unlikely – as unreal, by now, as his own fabrications. This didn't lessen the pain, however. For some reason she felt lonelier now than she'd felt in the past, before she met him. And, weirdly, more elderly. She'd been shunted forward a notch, nearer to her dad.

She remembered her father talking about the loneliness of old age. 'It's one of the things, like flatulence and phlegm, they don't warn you about.'

He'd talked about this a great deal – more, in fact, than he talked about missing their mother. Maybe he'd been less prepared for it.

That afternoon she walked to the abandoned factory

site. After the recent heatwave the pond had shrunk. The remaining water was blackish and choked with crisp packets. There was no sign of the newts.

In fact it hardly seemed the same pond. Had it all been a dream? Farida the laughing wife, her white jeans smudged with mud? Robert the successful novelist? She, the woman whose wrinkled body was actually desired? That joy they'd felt – was it as illusory as everything else seemed to be?

Phoebe gazed at the expanse of concrete. Poor me, poor Robert, she thought. Our dreams had been born in sheds, his in a garden and mine in a wood, and both had turned out to be simply a figment of our imaginations. A puff of sound and fury, signifying nothing. A few words from Mandy, and they were demolished.

She tried to be cheerful, for her father's sake. She doubted, however, that he noticed anything was wrong. His world had shrunk to his and Mandy's small doings. The trips to Lidl, a new girl at the shop. The ever-more-elaborate bird feeders, which he told her about in great – and indeed boring – detail. Her dad, *boring*. Who would believe it? The solipsism of the elderly is something she hadn't anticipated, not with a man of his calibre. How had the mighty fallen. And it was happening so fast. Each time she visited, he seemed to have slipped further away.

Of course, he had always been preoccupied. His brain was fizzing with ideas, he was bound up with his work. Throughout her childhood the phone was ringing; it was their mother who had time to listen. But there were moments that she remembered so vividly, when he was with her, full-beam. *I'm so glad you're six and we can have a proper conversation.* And she still had glimpses of this, even now. It was just that these moments were becoming increasingly rare. He was slipping away from her, and becoming Mandy's. She was his world, now.

Of course Phoebe didn't resent it. Of *course* not. But then something happened that changed it all.

The weather had broken and it was pouring with rain.

'Nice weather for the ducks,' Mandy said. Her father laughed. Was he being ironic or had he never heard this before?

Phoebe had brought some flowers – they never had flowers in the house – and Mandy went into the kitchen to put them in a vase. Her father was wearing the tracksuit bottoms and his beige cardigan; today he looked like an elderly publican. It was hard to believe he had once been a professor of physics. She sat down next to him and took his hand. There were a couple of sticking-plasters on it. His skin was paper-thin; it tore easily and took forever to heal.

'How's your week been?' she asked.

'Graham next door's bought a new car. They've got two now, him and Janet.'

'Any jaunts?'

He looked vague, for a moment. 'I think we went *somewhere.*'

'I rang on Wednesday but couldn't get a reply, so I presumed you were out.'

He raised his voice. 'Where did we go, Mandy?'

'Oh, just to Oxford.' She came in with the vase. 'These are ever so pretty. Can you tell me what they are? I don't know anything about flowers.'

'Did you drive past our old house?' Phoebe asked her father. They had lived in North Oxford. 'Someone said they've built a big new extension where Robert and I had our sandpit.'

He shook his head. 'We just went straight in and out again. Had to see my solicitors.'

'That's not true, pet,' said Mandy. 'We had a lovely cream tea in that hotel.' She turned to Phoebe. 'You know the one, the famous one, it's got a lovely lounge and they had jam in proper little glass jars, Tiptree, not any old garbage.'

She paused, breathing heavily. Her doughy face was flushed.

'You saw your solicitor?' Phoebe asked her dad. 'Nothing wrong?'

'No, nothing at all.'

'Where would you like these flowers?' asked Mandy. 'On the table or in front of the window?' She turned to Phoebe. 'Are you still doing the paintings? You're so clever. I can't draw for toffee but my friend Maureen, she got the art prize for our whole year. She got a book of pictures by Constable.' She babbled away, shuffling the flowers around in the vase. 'I wasn't good at anything at school. Well, I was good at swimming but that was it. I wasn't clever like you and Robert. I only got three O levels.'

'You're very good at looking after grumpy old men,' said her dad. 'That's the main thing.'

Phoebe wasn't listening. *Solicitor.* She felt that sinking sensation again, this time deepened with a darker suspicion. Why on earth had he gone to see his solicitor?

She watched Mandy ease him out of his chair and help him across the room. That flat in Droitwich; it was left to

127

her in somebody's will. Some old chap she'd been looking after.

Her dad went into the lavatory and closed the door. Mandy turned to the window, her glasses flashing in the sunshine. 'It's stopped raining,' she said. 'That's a blessing.' And she disappeared into the kitchen.

Why had her father gone to his solicitor, and why were they both being so evasive?

This time Phoebe brought along lunch. Mandy's salads were disheartening – beetroot bleeding into lettuce, slices of tasteless tomato, the sort of thing people used to eat before they knew better. Her father had never been a foodie but she couldn't bear him to spend the rest of his days eating this stuff when he had so few pleasures left. She remembered Rejoice and the maize-meal that turned his bowels to concrete.

So there she was, peeling foil from various containers while Mandy stood beside her, so near she could hear the woman breathing. Neither of them spoke. Phoebe wondered if Mandy knew what she was thinking. When she was upstairs, eating those biscuits, had she been ferreting out his will? Had she been putting pressure on him to alter it? When Phoebe had mentioned his solicitor, Mandy had hastily changed the subject. And there had been an odd atmosphere in the room, as if Dad, too, was being purposefully vague. Phoebe had caught them exchanging glances.

Or was it all her imagination?

'What's this when it's at home?'

Phoebe jumped.

'Tabbouleh,' she said. 'From the deli in Knockton.'

'Foreign, is it?'

'Sort of Middle Eastern.'

Mandy yanked open the cutlery drawer. 'I expect you've been all over the world.'

'Here and there, I suppose. Not as much as Dad.'

'Well, he was an important person.'

Phoebe looked at Mandy but her face was bland.

'He was away a lot,' she said.

'Did your mum go with him?'

'Sometimes. When Robert and I were older and had left home.'

'I expect she wanted to keep him on the leash.'

'What?'

'Well, she wasn't stupid, from what I've heard.'

'What do you mean?'

'He was a bit of a ladies' man, wasn't he?' Mandy looked out of the window. 'Shall I dry the seats? Then we could eat in the garden.'

Phoebe stared at her. 'What do you mean, *ladies' man*?'

'Oops.' She raised her eyebrows. 'Didn't you know?'

'He wasn't like that! What on earth are you talking about?'

Mandy shrugged. 'I thought you knew. I mean, your mum not being keen on that sort of thing.'

'What sort of thing?'

'Never mind.'

Phoebe's hands were shaking. She put down the glass. 'I don't think you should talk about them like that. And it's not true. They were utterly devoted. I should know, I'm their bloody daughter.'

'Sorry, sorry I spoke.'

Mandy picked up the tray and kicked open the door into the garden. Phoebe followed her out.

'Who told you this rubbish?'

Mandy put the tray on the table. 'Could you get a cloth, love?'

'Who told you? Dad?'

'Listen, love, forget it. I talked out of turn. I'm such a blabbermouth.' She gave her arm a slap. 'Naughty Mandy.'

For a moment Phoebe was too angry to speak. She glanced at the French windows. Dad sat there, in the shadowy room.

'Anyway, it's none of my business,' Mandy said.

'Exactly. So let's just shut up, shall we?'

Suddenly Mandy put her arms around her and gave her a hug. How tightly she held her! Too surprised to move, Phoebe sank into her soft flesh.

'Please don't kick me out,' Mandy muttered into her hair. 'I love you all – I just speak as I find. It's always got me into trouble. Please say you forgive me.'

Phoebe nodded and tried to disentangle herself but Mandy held her in her grip.

'Pretty please?' she mumbled.

'Yes,' Phoebe lied, and Mandy released her.

Phoebe drove home in a daze. Clouds chased across the sky. A storm was brewing and the wind battered her car as she drove along the motorway.

How could Mandy say things like that about her parents' marriage? What right did she have to even *hint* at some sort of infidelity? It seemed extraordinarily presumptuous, to say the least. And just blurting it out – how weird was that? Her father might have charmed women but he was no adulterer. Why had Mandy tried to poison her mind?

A vast lorry passed, shaking Phoebe's car. She seemed to be crawling along in the slow lane. Was Mandy trying to prove something – that she knew her father better than his own children, that she was privy to his secrets? Was she just being spiteful? Jealous? Maybe so sexually frustrated herself that her fevered imagination had started to make stuff up?

The only other explanation was that her dad *had* said something. His personality was going through a subtle change; they had all noticed it. There was the memory loss, of course, and the growing vagueness. Nowadays he even forgot the names of his grandchildren. But his very character was altering. There was that bewilderment in his eyes, a kind of wariness, which had grown more apparent over the past weeks. It seemed to have been triggered by the destruction of his love-seat. He had grown more querulous and confused, more irrationally angry. More frightened.

All these were early signs of dementia, of course. The dreaded word they didn't like to mention. Another sign, she'd read, was sexual disinhibition. Maybe her dad had been making sexually inappropriate remarks to Mandy, or bragging to her. This seemed difficult to imagine with her darling father, but age can have a coarsening effect on even the most civilised of minds.

Or maybe it was Mandy herself who was going mad.

When Phoebe got home she discovered there had been a power cut, and the High Street was plunged into darkness. Sodden from her dash across the yard, she blundered into the kitchen. The storm rattled the windowpanes as if it was giving the house a shake. She pictured it wrenched from its foundations and lifted, spinning, into the sky.

Her own moorings had been loosened; she felt alone, and utterly adrift. Had her father really been unfaithful? Sixty-four years of marriage; it was not beyond the bounds of possibility, especially for such an irresistible man. Maybe he *had* briefly strayed. If so, he'd been like every man with whom she had ever been involved.

But she didn't want him to be like that. Not her dad. Surely he wasn't the sort? And what on earth had Mandy meant about her mother? She was a cool woman – severe, sometimes – but that hardly meant she was frigid.

Phoebe felt her childhood shifting beneath her. It was deeply disturbing, feeling the doubt spreading like poison into the past. How dare Mandy blunder into her family life like this and spread such stupid rumours? Maybe it was a class resentment thing and she wanted to prick their bubble of privilege. And then, almost worse, she'd back-tracked, all sickly-sweet and huggy-huggy. Cloying. Phoebe could still feel her pillowy flesh; the scent of TCP from dressing her father's wound.

Trapped in her grip, Phoebe had hated her. Hated her with a fury, for the very first time. But then she'd calmed down. *Mustn't take offence.* Because how could they possibly cope without her?

So they'd had lunch. Afterwards, while her father had his nap, Phoebe did some vigorous work in the garden, wrenching out weeds and slashing the nettles, taking out her aggression on the plants. It was surprisingly therapeutic. Then they had tea and played Boggle. Anyone looking through the windows – no longer possible, with the net curtains – they would have seen a charming and peaceful scene. And her father, of course, had been completely unaware that anything had happened.

Sunday night and Knockton was dead, there was nobody around to come to her rescue. Phoebe rummaged blindly in the kitchen drawer, feeling for some candles. In the fridge, her food silently rotted. Shamefully, she longed for a man, even somebody elderly and boring from the internet. The sort of man who took photos of potholes and sent them to the council. The sort of man she deserved.

Just for a moment she envied her father: that he was cared for day and night, that there was another warm human body in the house. She'd even put up with Mandy, not to feel so utterly alone.

The next day her brother phoned.

'You won't believe this,' he said. 'I've just found out that Dad went to see his solicitor last week, and changed his will.'

Robert

Robert had a private income. So what? Plenty of people did, it was nothing to be ashamed of. The money came from his mother's side of the family – coal mines near Stockport, long ago. It wasn't a vast amount, but enough to save him from stacking shelves in Tesco, which at his age would be a bit tragic. Farida was the money-earner in their marriage and, now his hopes of a novel were dashed, would continue to be for the foreseeable. But she too had had the benefit of a hefty leg-up in the past, thanks to her father. They had both been fortunate.

But pity the poor kids. They'd been priced right out of the property market. London had become a pension-pot for foreign investors – Chinese, Malays, Russians, they were all at it, buying up flats in hideous skyscrapers that cast their neighbourhoods into darkness and destroyed their communities. Young people hadn't a hope in hell of getting onto the housing ladder. Even rentals were way out of their reach.

So he and Farida had been determined to help their children; it was one of the few topics on which they agreed. Alice wanted to buy into a flat-share in Homerton – once a Slough of Despond but now apparently a hipster hotspot. They needed to sort out the legal side, so Robert rang Jonty Cummings, his family's solicitor in Oxford. They had been to the same school and had remained friends; nothing bonds two fellows like wanking together behind the bike sheds.

Jonty was a jovial chap and, for a solicitor, gratifyingly indiscreet. After they'd discussed Alice's flat he said that he'd seen Robert's father only the other day.

'Looking quite spry, I must say. Had a carer-person with him. Quite heroically plain, isn't she? Big knockers, though.' He paused. 'And bigger tummy.' Robert asked him why his father had come to see him and he replied breezily: 'Oh, to fiddle with his will.'

Robert's heart hammered against his ribs. 'Er, in what respect exactly?'

'Ha! My lips are sealed.'

Robert rang off. *Oh God.*

His suspicions had been lurking, of course. The Droitwich business, the bedroom business. Mandy's sometimes weird behaviour and probing questions. But the confirmation still shocked him to his bones. In fact he felt physically sick.

Farida was in the kitchen unpacking an Ocado delivery. He heard the clack-clack of her heels as she walked from fridge to larder and back again, to and fro on the limestone floor. Her shoes beat a military tattoo that rallied his thoughts into marching order. *I must find out more, I must find out more.* I must talk to my sister.

He went into the living room, out of earshot, and phoned Phoebe. Her gasp was gratifying. Suddenly they were conspirators. Their differences were forgotten in the face of the common enemy.

She told him she'd seen their father the day before, and that Mandy had behaved oddly. 'They were *both* odd, as if they had something to hide. I was going to ring you about it but there was a power cut, and then it came back on and I had to dash about reprogramming all those bloody lights winking everywhere. He mentioned the solicitors but Mandy shut him up, and then she started hinting that he'd had extra-marital affairs.'

'*What?*'

'I know, I know. I wasn't going to tell you because it was so ridiculous. It was just mischief-making. The woman's borderline bonkers. I think it comes from sexual depriv-ation. I mean, who would even *contemplate* it?'

'Big knockers, though.'

'Rob!'

It was then that he had an idea.

The references.

He ran upstairs and rummaged in his desk for the *Mandy* file.

Phoebe burst out laughing. 'Are you mad?'

'We just visit, and drop it casually into the conversation.'

'What – *Did your dead mother leave Mandy anything in her will?*'

'We'll be subtler than that.'

'How?'

'We'll think of something.'

'Why can't we just phone?'

'We need to see the whites of their eyes. Come on, sis, it's only Enfield.'

'Huh, it's only Enfield to *you*. It's two hundred miles to *me*.'

But he could tell she was wavering. For all her faults,

Phoebe had always been up for adventure. Alarmingly so, in her youth.

And what did they have to lose? It wasn't as if they had anything better to do. Robert had been brooding recently on the pointlessness of their creative endeavours, Phoebe's as much as his own. As Mandy had tactlessly remarked, what was the use of glasses you couldn't actually drink out of? As uselessly useless as his useless novel.

Mandy has been a godsend, wrote Rowena Gayle from Enfield. Of the three referees, this woman had been the only one who'd responded to his email. She sounded mildly curious that they wanted to see her, but perfectly amenable.

So now he and Phoebe were walking up the path of a substantial house in Thorpe Avenue, Enfield.

'Stop giggling,' he hissed.

'It just seems so funny. Shall we ring the bell and run away, like we did when we were little?'

It did seem preposterous. Robert's nerves were tingling. He suddenly felt flooded with love for his fellow detective, who knew him better than anyone in the world. Phoebe had smartened herself up for this visit – loose red trousers, white top and cardigan, her bushy hair pulled back in a ponytail. Nothing hippie about her today. She could be carrying a clipboard.

As it turned out, they needn't have worried. Rowena Gayle was visibly drunk and, once she started talking, there was no stopping her. They sat in her conservatory while she poured them large glasses of wine and dismissed their polite commiserations with a *hurrumph*.

'My mother was a bitch. An evil cow. She's been dead for two years and every morning I thank my lucky stars she's

gone.' She lit a cigarette. 'Sent us all to boarding school –
my dad was a wimp – sent us away so she could flounce
about having sex with half the married men in Middlesex.
Is it any wonder that I have abandonment issues?'

Robert could see that his sister was warming to her; she
had always been drawn to neurotic women. Rowena was
gimlet-eyed, sallow, and greyhound-thin. She'd recently
retired from the Department of Work and Pensions.

They asked about Mandy, who had looked after the old
woman for the last few months of her life.

'It was pretty hellish because she kept telling lies.'

Phoebe stiffened. 'Lies?'

'Sneaky, nasty lies. Mischief-making.'

Robert glanced at his sister. Her eyes flickered to his.
This was getting interesting.

It turned out, however, that Rowena was referring to her
mother, who had dementia. She had nothing but praise for
Mandy.

'We all loved her. She was a godsend. Endlessly patient,
putting up with Mother's rages. Taking her out on little
trips. Nothing was too much trouble. She told us not to
worry, she said, *I'll take care of everything, that's what I'm
here for.* The pain management, the morphine. You see,
soon after she arrived my mother's condition worsened and
she went downhill very quickly. So we took Mandy at her
word and left her to it. She was all alone with my mother
when she died, she said it was very peaceful, which was
more than that witch deserved.'

'So you had no problems with her?'

Rowena shook her head, smoke leaking from her nostrils. 'She binged on my biscuits but who could blame her?

Used to smuggle them into her room and leave crumbs around.'

'Did she discuss any of the other people she looked after?'

'Sometimes. An old lady who imagined she was living in a hotel – she mentioned her. I suppose I should have checked her references but to be perfectly honest I was just so glad to have her, I never bothered.'

'Did she ever behave oddly, sort of nosing around?'

'Not really,' Rowena said. 'Do you have problems with her, is this what this is all about?'

Suddenly, a familiar chirrup came from the room behind them.

'Blimey, did she buy your mother a clock?' Robert asked.

Rowena nodded. 'A barmy bird thing. Thinking of my mother's state of mind, it should've had a cuckoo.' She snorted with laughter and started coughing. 'I must take it to Oxfam.'

'I know it sounds weird,' said Phoebe, 'but did your mother leave anything to Mandy in her will?'

Rowena was too drunk to be startled. 'God, no.' She drained her glass. 'Though, now you mention it, my mother *did* try to change it. She was always threatening to; it was a power thing. But I have no idea what she had in mind – in what was *left* of her mind – and the solicitor dismissed it as invalid.'

After a large glass of wine Robert's head was swimming. He gazed around at the bamboo furniture, the heaped cushions. Beyond the conservatory stretched an impressive garden – vast lawn, gazebo, weeping willow.

Rowena watched him. 'It's all tainted money, my family's

money, all this.' She waved her hand, ash falling from her cigarette. 'It came from the *Titanic*.'

'The *Titanic*?'

'My great-grandfather worked for Lloyd's, the underwriters. He gambled on the insurance – I don't know how he did it. But when the ship sank he never had to work again.' She drained the bottle into her glass. 'Do you know something, my dear new friends? That money caused nothing but misery. Greed, lies, divorce, family feuds. All from fifteen hundred drowned souls.' She viciously stubbed out her cigarette. 'Maybe we deserved it.'

Robert and Phoebe sat on the tube. It was Saturday and some match was on; the carriage was rammed with bellowing fans, bumping into their knees and swigging cans of lager. They could smell the testosterone.

'That was interesting,' said Phoebe. She pulled out the band and shook her hair free.

Robert wondered if she was thinking the same thing as him. They had been remarkably in tune recently.

Soon after she arrived my mother's condition worsened and she went downhill quickly.

Their father was deteriorating, no doubt about that.

He was right, because then Phoebe said: 'Remember what Alice told us, about that weird conversation in the loo?'

She looked at Robert, her eyebrows raised. The pitiless glare of the carriage drained the colour from her face.

Morphine. Pills. Who knew? Anything could be going on in that cottage in the middle of nowhere.

What if Mandy was not an angel of mercy, but an angel of death?

Once lodged, suspicions are impossible to shift. Not until something happens that proves they're groundless.

Farida knew nothing of this. Robert hadn't even told her about the visit to Enfield. He could imagine her shrivelling response. *Don't be an idiot. You two, honestly! Cooking up this stuff just because you feel guilty. So he's left her something in his will, so what? Doesn't she deserve it? If he was MY father he'd be living here with us. We've got masses of room; he'd even have his own ensuite. Isn't that what families are supposed to be about? And you call MANDY weird.*

Farida the human drone, on target as always. Gazing at him, eyebrows raised, head tilted.

His dreams were upsetting, those hot summer nights. He dreamed his shed had disappeared, leaving a patch of mud scored with tyre tracks. In its place was his parents' love-seat, the original one with the delicate legs. He knew Farida had put it there to disguise the destruction of his hut. This was so real that he woke up and rolled over to accuse her, but the bed was empty: she had already gone to work. That morning there she was on the TV, fronting a report on a million starving Sudanese, their own huts stretching to infinity.

He thought of his dad at the newt pond, longing to die. For millions it came too early but for him the moment was right. If only it could be that simple. Robert's friends were already talking about Dignitas, and taking control of their own extinction. He had never been a hippie but that sixties vibe was travelling through the decades like a guinea pig swallowed by a python. *We changed the way we live, so now we're changing the way we die.*

So how did his father feel, who was a generation older? Did he really want to eke out his last years in that stifling room scratching away at his scratch-card, his final gamble and one he was bound to lose?

Maybe he and Mandy had an understanding.

Maybe she was killing him, very slowly so it would never be detected, in order to get her hands on his money. Presuming, of course, that she had become so indispensable to him, so deeply loved, that he had changed his will in her favour.

Or so confused she had persuaded him.

Or none of this had happened and both he and his sister had diseased minds. There were some people in the world who were simply good. They might have a noddy dog in their car but that simply meant they weren't his type. And what was so great about his type anyway? Nobody he knew was a purely good person. Least of all himself.

With some people it seemed to be simple. They were loved, and loved in return. So it went down the generations. For most of them, however, it was more complicated. He remembered what Rowena said about her mother. 'Even when she was dead the bitch nearly killed me. She'd left instructions for her ashes to be scattered off the rocks in Cornwall where she used to go on holiday. So I clambered down with the urn and slipped. It was a sheer drop and I bloody nearly drowned. Which, in the circumstances, would have been appropriate.' She'd snorted with laughter and lit another cigarette. 'Our family's comeuppance at last, after a hundred years.'

*

The next time, he and Phoebe visited their father together. They didn't discuss this; it just seemed inevitable. So many scenarios were swimming about in their heads that it seemed important for them both to be there, supporting each other, watching out for signs that might confirm their suspicions.

Robert was feeling empty. His novel had gone; he hadn't realised how central it had been to his life. All those characters he'd once loved; it was like having a cage of dead rabbits in the corner of the room. By now they were starting to smell. Farida's lack of surprise had made it even more mortifying; she'd made it clear that she'd suspected all along he couldn't hack it.

He felt his father disappearing too – losing his personality, losing his wits, losing his interests, one by one, and retreating into his final refuge: Mandyworld. His connection to his children was loosening; Mandy had him now. Quite honestly, he seemed fonder of her than he was of them, his own flesh and blood.

No wonder Robert was depressed. And now his own children had deserted him. Alice had gone to New Zealand for six months, some water-sports thing. Jack was on holiday, driving across America with his girlfriend, and wasn't responding to emails.

Farida was – well, Farida.

God, he longed for a dog.

So now he and Phoebe were parking their cars outside the church. Their father's lane was blocked off because the village fête was being held in the nearby field. As they walked to his cottage a Tannoy announced the sack race. Robert looked over the hedge. The sparse local population had been bolstered by the weekenders who were patronising the fête's retro charms before legging it back to W11. He glimpsed a couple of their ghastly children engrossed with their smartphones under a sagging string of bunting.

Each year a minor – sometimes very minor – celebrity opened the fête. Five years earlier it had been Farida. This had been considered something of a coup and his parents' standing in the village had shot up. Farida had been peerlessly professional – friendly, engaged, talking to the scouts and the old dears, doing the raffle, staying until the bitter end. How intensely he had loved her, then. He remembered it as one of the happiest days in his marriage. It could happen, even now. Joy unbidden, like that moment with the newts.

And now here was his dad, complaining about what he called *the blithering noise*. 'Just seen a little girl walking across my flowerbeds, bold as brass, dressed as some kind of tart.'

'It was a flamenco costume, petal,' said Mandy.

'High heels, anyway. At her age!'

Dad, oh Dad, where have you gone? When did you morph into Disgusted of Chipping Norbury?

Robert hadn't seen his father for three weeks. Several small, purple nodules had appeared on his face. His eyes were rheumy and sunken. He kept looking at his watch, as if he had an important appointment and was waiting for everyone to clear off. His knee jiggled.

Robert could see that Phoebe was equally shocked by his condition. Earlier, she'd suggested they took him out for lunch but Mandy said he wasn't up to it and now they could see why. Jaunts of any kind were out of the question; that trip to Wales, only a month ago, would be unthinkable in his present state. Was this just a bad day, Robert wondered, or was he indeed going downhill fast?

There was a queer, constrained atmosphere over lunch. The old man ate little. Mandy's cooking was hardly inspiring but he'd always had a healthy appetite.

'You've done us proud,' he told her, as he toyed with a piece of liver sausage. *Done us proud* was another phrase he'd caught from her.

Mandy beamed at him. She was wearing a vast yellow T-shirt with the slogan: *I've Been to Chessington Zoo*. Her slabs of arms were pink from the sun.

'Mandy's become the mainstay of the village, haven't you, love?' James gazed at her with devotion. 'Baking cakes for the other decrepits, organising the jumble sale. I don't know how they managed without you.'

'Where I come from, it's just what we do. We look out for each other.' Mandy wiped a blob of grease from his chin. 'My mum said that happiness is like coke.'

'Coke?' Phoebe perked up.

'It's something you get as a by-product of something else,' said Mandy. 'Like coal.'

His father nodded. 'Aldous Huxley said that.'

'Aldous Huxley?' asked Mandy. 'What team does he play for?' They both chuckled; it was obviously one of their jokes.

Robert felt a stab of irritation. Music drifted in from the field: Frank Ifield's 'I Remember You'. Suddenly he was back in his childhood. It was sports day and he was competing in the egg-and-spoon race. He could still feel the glazed, wooden egg wobbling in its spoon as he ran to the finishing line.

'I might not have played for a team,' he told his dad. 'Unlike Aldous Huxley. But I *did* win the egg-and-spoon race back in 1964. The only thing I've ever won in my life. I remember looking around, I thought you'd be there. But there was only mum.'

'Really, is that true?' asked Dad.

'Children remember these things,' he said peevishly. 'Especially when you'd promised to come.'

A small silence followed his outburst. It was stiflingly hot; sweat dampened his armpits. Frank was still singing but his father wasn't listening. Robert thought: under the charm you're a ruthless old bastard.

'Strange, isn't it,' his dad mused. 'We hardly remember anything from the first four or five years of our life; it disappears as if it never existed. So all the things one does, as a parent, with a small child – the playgrounds, the stories, all that effort one makes – it happens in a fog of forgetfulness. We might never have bothered. They've done studies on the subject, most fascinating.'

'I'm not talking about studies, I'm talking about *me*!' Robert's voice rose. 'A little boy, constantly let down. Phoebe, too. *All that effort one makes* – you didn't make any effort at all! And it's still going on, after all these years. You haven't asked us a single thing about what we've been up to.'

He stopped, breathing heavily. His father looked mildly taken aback. Phoebe stared at him, astonished.

'Anyone for apple crumble?' asked Mandy. 'Robert, could you help me bring out the plates?'

In the kitchen she swung round to face him, bumping against the sink. 'You shouldn't talk to your father like that. You're a grown man.'

'You have no idea about us and Dad.'

'I know your father pretty well. Every orifice. Which is more than can be said for you.'

'I don't want to know his orifices.'

'Yes, that's what you pay *me* for.' She glared at him through her glasses. Her face was sheeny with perspiration. 'Whinge, whinge, that's all you do, you and your sister.' Her voice dropped to a hiss. 'This isn't about *you,* it's about *him*. When you come to visit, it's *him* you should be thinking of, but you just moan. Haven't you got anything better to do? Nobody's perfect. Why don't you get a life?'

For a moment Robert couldn't speak. Outside, they started playing 'My Very Good Friend, the Milkman'. He suddenly felt exhausted. 'You really shouldn't talk to me like that.'

'I speak as I find—'

'Do stop saying that—'

'And it's as plain as a pikestaff. You're ever so unhappy, you and your sister. You've had bugger all else to do except sit on your bottoms examining your feelings and where's it got you? No bloody where. That's the problem with money. In my family we had nothing, *nothing*, we had no choice except to roll up our sleeves and get on with it. That's what you lot don't understand, you with your silver spoons in your mouths. You've never been poor. If you're poor you have no sodding choices at all.' She pushed back her damp fringe. 'Pardon my language.' The funny thing was, she didn't seem angry or even bitter. She just seemed despairing.

'Wow.'

Robert turned. Phoebe had joined them. She gazed at Mandy, eyebrows raised.

'I'm sorry,' said Mandy, 'but I speak as—'

'Do shut up.'

After this extraordinary outburst Mandy seemed to deflate. She leaned against the sink, breathing heavily. Outside, the music had stopped.

'Your dad misses you,' said Mandy. 'He talks about you all the time. You say he neglected you, he wasn't there for you. Well, now it's payback time because *you're* neglecting *him*.'

Neither of them spoke. Robert gazed at the parched surface of the apple crumble. Blackened juice had seeped through the cracks.

'I know you don't like me,' Mandy said. 'I can't do anything about that.'

'That's not true,' said Phoebe weakly.

'But let me tell you something else.' Mandy turned to Robert. 'I know I'm speaking out of turn and you'll like me even less now, but I've seen you with your wife and I can't help noticing things.'

'What things?'

'That you're ever so unhappy. Your dad was blessed with a good marriage but some people aren't so lucky.' She paused. 'I've been single all my life and it's not so bad. Honest it isn't. You should pluck up your courage and give it a go. And now I'll shut up.'

Robert was gobsmacked. He gazed at a list of words his father had pinned to the wall: 'ANTELOPE. MELLIFLUOUS. GRAHAM/JANET.' His *aide memoires*.

'Goodness,' said Phoebe at last. 'You really do speak as you find.'

Mandy picked up the dish of crumble. 'Anyway, at least I've brought you two together.'

'What do you mean?'

She looked at them. 'You used to needle each other all the time, but now you've got *me* to hate you're getting on like a house on fire.' She pushed open the door with her foot. 'Coming!' she called.

Phoebe

The gloves were off. Mandy thought they were spoilt brats who had abandoned their father so they could dick around doing useless stuff nobody wanted to buy. Moaning minnies who didn't appreciate how privileged they were. Rubbish at love, too, what with her, Phoebe's, taste for spineless stoners and Robert's marriage to a chilly ballbreaker. Altogether a waste of space, and snotty with it.

By implication, it was people like Mandy who were the bedrock of society. Hard-working, selfless and perennially cheerful, people who did the dirty work and mopped up the mess. The invisible people, without whom the rest of the world would fall to pieces. People who worked for a pittance, caring for their fellow human beings. People with hearts.

Weirdly enough, Phoebe wasn't offended. In fact she found it curiously bracing. When you're an adult it's rare to be attacked; you choose your friends because they agree with you and you agree with them. Open warfare is saved for your nearest and dearest – in other words, your family.

So Mandy's words had made her feel strangely intimate with her, almost familial. There was no denying, however, that the woman had been staggeringly rude. She'd crashed through the fourth wall of what should be a professional relationship – she was their employee, for God's sake – and put them in an impossible situation.

Should they sack her? Their father would be heartbroken. And would they find another person who could cater to his increasingly complex needs? And wouldn't it be a rather petty thing to do – to punish Mandy just because she'd over-stepped the mark and told them some home truths?

Because, of course, there *was* truth in what she said. It pained Phoebe to admit it. Mandy was a lot beadier than they'd realised. She'd been watching them, clocking them. Disapproving of them, from her position of virtue. Phoebe had seen that look in her eyes, when she was blandly chatting about this and that.

To be perfectly honest, thought Phoebe, I don't think she likes us at all.

Robert was angrier than she was. 'What a bloody cheek!' he'd said as they walked to their cars. 'I didn't hire her to tell me to divorce my wife.'

The trouble was, Phoebe secretly agreed with her. Farida hadn't made her brother happy. In fact she didn't think Farida was that happy herself. Undermining one's spouse is an exhausting process and takes its toll on both of you. And Phoebe suspected that her constant make-overs and renovations were a sign of a deeper malaise. Robert had hinted that their sex life was practically non-existent. Per-haps it was true, and their marriage had worn itself out. Now the children had left home this might be the time to jack it in and start afresh.

Buffy, her local hotelier, had form in these matters. Phoebe found his breezy cynicism a welcome relief. His favourite saying was, *I don't think I'll get married again.*

I'll just find a woman I don't like and give her a house. He loved discussing this sort of thing and recently mused, when they were drinking in his kitchen: 'In my experience, relationships always last, proportionally, a third longer than they should. In a nine-year-marriage, say, it'd be the final three years. We're too cowardly, too kind, too lazy, too terrified of being alone to do the decent thing and put it out of its misery. Trust me, I know.' They couldn't all be as lucky as her parents.

Phoebe was mulling over this the next day while she was out delivering 'Stop the Supermarket' leaflets. The weather had broken; bruised thunderclouds were building up in the west. On the TV that morning Farida had warned of heavy rain and possible flooding and they'd run their usual item on the lack of contingency plans. Just now, however, the air was heavily humid. Phoebe had checked on the newt pond but it had shrunk still smaller and there was no sign of life. Maybe some kids had fished out the newts, who knew?

There were six people delivering leaflets and she had been assigned the outlying properties because she had an electric bike. All her life she would remember that moment – the moment when fate intervened, and took any decision about Mandy out of her hands.

She was half a mile out of town, cycling down the hill towards a cluster of cottages deep in the valley. Next to them was a vast new poultry farm, itself the subject of a local campaign. Phoebe suspected that the workers there would be only too happy to have a supermarket in town, and hoped nobody would be around to shout at her.

As she freewheeled down the lane, her mobile rang. She slewed to a halt. It wasn't a number she recognised.

A man's voice came on the line. 'Is that James Wentworth's daughter?' His voice was shaking. 'This is Graham, your father's neighbour. I'm afraid I have some terrible news.'

The phone went dead. Phoebe tried to ring back but the signal had gone.

Within ten minutes she was crashing through the door of her house. She rushed to the landline phone, to ring Graham back, but when she checked her mobile for his number the screen was black. She'd run out of battery.

She knew Mandy's number, of course. With trembling fingers she rang her mobile, and then the landline. Nothing, just the answerphones. She rang her brother but there was no reply there, either. Even Farida wasn't responding.

She'd wasted fifteen minutes trying to make contact with somebody, anybody. She left messages for them, grabbed her bag and rushed out, stumbling over her bike where it lay abandoned in the yard. And then she was in her car, driving east.

Was her father lying there, dead, and Mandy too distraught to answer the phone? Or was she in the ambulance, or at the hospital, and unable to get a signal?

Maybe Graham had discovered him. Maybe Mandy was out and Graham had dropped in, for some reason or other, and found him dead. Maybe her dad had collapsed in the garden and Graham had seen him through the window.

Her father was dead. That was her only certainty.

And it was their fault, hers and Robert's. His attack on their father *had* been shocking. Neither of them had ever talked to him like that before. It had triggered a heart attack. A stroke.

There was a rumble of thunder and it started to rain. Outside Cheltenham she got stuck in a traffic jam. Her heart was pounding. Should she go straight to the hospital – it would be the one in Oxford, the John Radcliffe, wouldn't it? Or should she go to her father's house? The sky was so dark that drivers had switched on their lights. Traffic passing in the other direction sent up spumes of water. Her windscreen wipers slewed to and fro, *he's dead, he's dead*. She inched forward, the heavens releasing their torrents of tears.

He's dead, she thought, and I haven't said goodbye. This rain-lashed scene, this banal dual carriageway with an Eddie Stobart lorry thundering past in the opposite direction, the car in front with its children grimacing at her through the window, was a world without her father in it.

In an instant, everything had changed. We know it's bound to happen but nothing prepares us for the reality, nothing at all.

When Phoebe arrived at her father's cottage the ambulance was just pulling away. Its siren wasn't on. This, of course, was all the confirmation she needed. Nor was she surprised that it had been there for so long; she knew it took hours for all the formalities. She'd missed him. No chance now for one last moment with him, alone. Just to stroke his hand and kiss him goodbye.

The front door was ajar. She parked, jumped out of the car and ran through the rain into the living room.

Her father sat on the sofa. Janet from next door was bringing him a cup of tea.

He looked up at Phoebe, his face ashen. 'Oh, darling, thank goodness you're here.'

She couldn't speak. She stared at him, the blood draining from her face.

'I'm afraid she's died,' he said.

'Who's died?'

'My daughter.' His voice broke. 'She was in the kitchen and I heard this noise. Then I went in and she'd collapsed on the floor.'

Phoebe sat down beside him and took his hand. 'It's all right, Dad. I'm here. *I'm* your daughter, remember?'

'She's my daughter.'

He sat there, heaving with sobs. The poor man was utterly disorientated.

'He means Mandy,' said Janet. 'They've just taken her away.'

In the midst of this confusion Phoebe felt a stab of jealousy. He actually thought of Mandy as his daughter. Was that because she'd been a better daughter to him than she herself had been?

'I'm so terribly sorry,' she said. 'It must have been the most awful shock. But I'm here now – your daughter, Phoebe, remember?'

'Of course I know who you are! I'm not senile.' He removed his hand. 'You don't understand. She's my daughter, sweetheart. We were both going to tell you when the time was right. And now it's too late.'

Robert

Robert and his father sat in silence. A chirrup came from the kitchen, where Phoebe was making sandwiches. The neighbours had long since gone.

He sat there, dizzy with nausea. His brain was going through a massive gear-shift; he could feel its cogs grinding. It was all he could do to lift his glass of whisky. He'd arrived soon after Phoebe and she'd told him the news. Outside, the rain lashed down.

Now Phoebe was coming in, her face blank, carrying the tray as if she were sleepwalking. She put it on the table. The armchair creaked as she sat down. They looked at the sandwiches.

'I'm afraid there was only tongue,' she said.

No way was he going to look at his father. He heard the sound of him swallowing and then the clunk as he put down his glass.

'I had no idea,' his father said. 'Not for a long time. Months, in fact. She knew who I was but I didn't know about her. It was quite a shock, as you could imagine.'

'Quite a shock,' said Phoebe. 'Yes.'

'That's when the love-seat broke,' he said. 'She sat down with me, in the garden, to tell me.'

'Why didn't she tell you straight away?' Robert demanded. 'Who was her mother? How did she find you?'

'Why didn't you tell *us*?' snapped Phoebe.

Their father raised his hands, as if to ward off a cloud of bees. 'Wait, wait, one thing at a time.' He took a breath. 'She loved her parents dearly. Her father had always known she wasn't his but brought her up as his own. But when they died, her parents, she had this urge to track me down.'

'Who was her mother?'

He paused. 'This . . . woman I knew.'

'Yes, we gather that,' said Phoebe. 'Who was she? Where did you meet her? How long did it go on for?'

She glared at him as if he were an errant child. He shifted in his seat.

'We met at a conference in Cardiff.'

'How? Who was she?'

'She worked for the caterers.'

'The caterers?'

'She was a waitress.' His face softened. For a moment it belonged to somebody else, not their father at all. 'Silver service,' he added with pride.

'How long did it go on for?' demanded Phoebe.

He paused. 'A while.'

'How long?'

'Does it really matter?'

'Of course it does! How long?'

'Four years.'

Robert and Phoebe stared at him, speechless. For the first time he looked sheepish.

'When was this? When we were children?'

He nodded.

'Was she married?'

He nodded.

'So you were both married.'

He nodded again.

'Where did you used to meet?'

He looked up. 'Do we really have to go on with this?'

'*Yes!*' Robert barked.

He dropped his gaze. The sandwiches lay untouched, their tongues poking out.

'A friend of her family had a caravan park in Crickhowell,' he said.

'What, near our cottage?'

He nodded.

'That's where you used to meet?'

Phoebe was thinking hard. Robert could almost feel it. So was he.

'Is that why you bought Haford?' he asked, at last.

'I wanted you to have holidays in the country,' their father said. 'To roam free.'

'Bullshit,' Robert said. 'That's why you bought it, wasn't it?'

Their father drained his whisky. His hand was trembling. 'Look, I really don't feel up to this. Not today, of all days.'

'Fuck how you feel,' Robert said.

'I've just lost my daughter—'

'Fuck that,' said Phoebe. 'You owe it to us. I presume our mother didn't know about your little trysts.'

'If that's what you want to call them.'

'What do you suggest?' Robert snapped. 'Your shags?'

He flinched. 'It wasn't like that!'

'What did you do, play Racing Demon?'

He took a breath. 'I mean, I was very much in love with her. And with your mother. I was horribly torn.'

Phoebe barked with laughter. 'Horribly torn!' Then she burst into tears.

'Oh, my dear . . .'

Their father tried to get up but she waved him away. 'Don't!'

'What was she called, this woman?' Robert asked.

'Stella.' That softened face again.

Stella.

'That's why you were always going away.'

'Not always,' he said. 'Sometimes it was work.'

'But sometimes – quite often – it wasn't,' Robert said. 'You were seeing *her*. Stella.'

A burst of birdsong came from the kitchen. God knew what time it was. The rain seemed to have stopped.

Phoebe pulled out a tissue and blew her nose.

'I'm so very sorry,' said their father. 'For everything.'

'If it wasn't for Mandy, we'd never have known,' Robert said.

'I expect not.' He raised his head and gazed at them with his bloodshot eyes. 'What I hope is that now you're older—'

'Actually pretty old,' snuffled Phoebe.

'Yes, but you'll always be my children, whatever age you are.' He paused. 'But now you're older and been through things yourself, you might understand.'

'Understand?'

'How terribly complicated everything is, when it comes to matters of the heart.'

'Not really,' Robert said. 'Not in this case.'

'Mum never knew?' asked Phoebe.

He shook his head.

'I expect you were very careful,' she said.

'I expect we were.'

There was a silence as the two of them reorganised their childhood. Robert could feel his sister's effortful re-examination of probably the same events. The phone calls. The absences.

'And when did Mandy come along?' she asked.

'After it was over. I didn't know Stella was pregnant.' He paused. 'Nor did she.'

'How did she know it wasn't her husband's?'

'Ken couldn't have children.'

Ken. It was all thickening up, horribly, into another par-allel life.

'And what did *he* have to say about it?' asked Phoebe.

'I don't know. As I said, it was over between us and I never saw her again. But Mandy told me he accepted her as his own child and simply loved her. By all accounts he was a very sweet man. A saint.'

'Who you betrayed for four years,' said Phoebe.

Their father sat slumped in his chair. He was old and ill and had just lost his daughter, they shouldn't be harangu-ing him like this. Robert was suddenly overcome with exhaustion but he could see that Phoebe had a hideous compulsion to persevere.

'So when they died, Mandy tracked you down,' she said.

He nodded. 'Through the internet.' They could see he was relieved to move on to this. 'Then she found out about the agency. She was already a registered carer, you see, she just signed on with them.'

'Why didn't she tell you straight away who she was?' Phoebe couldn't quite use the word *daughter.* Not yet.

'She thought it would give me a heart attack. The shock.

She said she just wanted to be with me, to get to know me and find out about me. After all, her real father was Ken.'

Robert thought of Mandy upstairs, rifling through his dad's letters and old photographs. Asking him and Phoebe questions about the past.

'But she did in the end,' said Phoebe. 'Tell you.'

Their father nodded. 'I had a little stroke, you see—'

'What?'

'Several little strokes, in fact.'

'Why didn't you tell us?'

He shrugged. 'You weren't here. I didn't want to worry you. They were only tiny.'

'*She* should have told us.'

'I told her not to. I didn't want to be a bore.'

'A *bore*?'

'A burden. Anyway, I was in good hands.'

Robert didn't know how to respond to this. Worried? Resentful? Neither did Phoebe. She got up and fetched the whisky bottle.

'So she thought I'd better know the truth,' said their father. 'Before it was too late.'

Robert remembered how he and Phoebe had noticed a change. The disorientation; the look in the old man's eyes. They'd thought it was the beginnings of dementia when in fact he was simply trying to cope with the hugest of secrets.

'Once I knew . . .' Their father paused. 'Once I knew, it seemed like the most natural thing in the world.'

Phoebe flinched, as if she'd been slapped.

The tactless old fool. Robert glared at him. 'So why did neither of you tell *us*?'

'It was up to her. She was going to, of course, but it was

never the right moment, she kept putting it off. She said to me once, "They've had you all their lives. It's my turn to have you now. Just for a little while." '

Phoebe unscrewed the whisky bottle. Their father held out his glass. His hands were trembling yet he was speaking with clarity, his old vagueness gone. Maybe it was a relief to tell the truth at last.

'And she was nervous,' he said.

Robert raised his eyebrows. '*Mandy*, nervous?'

'She said you were both so clever and sophisticated. She was worried you'd be horrified to find out who she was. That you'd be ashamed of her.'

'*What?*'

'She felt inferior.'

Phoebe looked astonished. 'I hope it was nothing we said.'

He shrugged. 'You don't need to *say* anything.'

Robert and Phoebe relapsed into silence. There were so many questions, yet there was no energy left. Not just now.

Their father looked grey, and so very old. The man had lost his daughter. Amidst all this, Robert kept forgetting. And they had found, and lost, a sister. Just now it was all too overwhelming to comprehend.

Phoebe

Phoebe and Robert stayed the night. One of them could have gone home, but home seemed strangely irrelevant – another country whose map, once they arrived there, would be utterly changed. Besides, they'd drunk too much whisky to drive.

And of course they couldn't leave their father alone. Not tonight, or for the foreseeable. They were the carers now.

They had no idea what this entailed, however, no idea at all. For it was a major operation. First their father had to be showered. He could get into the downstairs bathroom, with help, but he was too rocky on his legs to stand in the shower cubicle whilst soaping himself. Robert looked squeamish about this so Phoebe volunteered.

'I can still manage the lavatory part,' the old man said, to her relief. 'Peeing, I mean. Though Mandy has to help me when it comes to number twos.'

Wiping bottoms was just a job to her. Phoebe couldn't imagine doing such a thing, but already she was being shunted into intimacy with her father's body.

For she had never seen him naked. Sometimes in swimming trunks, decades ago, but now she was helping undress an elderly man whose face and hands were familiar but whose body was shockingly alien – grey skin peppered with moles, sagging breasts and stomach. Below its creases, beneath the sparse pubic hair, hung the adulterous penis that had brought her into the world. She caught the briefest glimpse of it as she helped him into the cubicle. If he was embarrassed, however, he was braving it out.

'One tries to retain one's last vestige of dignity,' he said. 'But, to be frank, it's rather a relief now it's gone.'

By now, no doubt, he was used to having his body man-handled. The very young and the very old have this in common. That Phoebe was doing it seemed to make little difference to him, or so he pretended. He held onto han-dles, fixed to the cubicle walls, as she soaped him with a sponge on a plastic stick. This must have been Mandy's invention, to stop herself getting wet. There was something of the crucifixion about this that was unsettling.

Afterwards, wrapped in a dressing gown, he sat on the lavatory while Phoebe dried his legs. His ankles were swol-len and blotchy due to poor circulation. First she had to massage them with moisturiser, then massage his feet with another cream, and anoint the yellowing shards of his toe-nails with fungicidal jelly. Then she rubbed lotion into the skin of his buttocks, fragile as tissue paper, which had become sore from all the sitting.

During this he was silent. No doubt he was remembering Mandy and her expert hands – that professional caress that morphed into a daughterly one. How odd it must have been, for him. Odd for Phoebe, too, exploring his body like this. Totally unerotic, yet not dissimilar to the first time she'd had sex.

'I remember bathing you,' he said, making her jump.

'Did you?'

He nodded. 'You and Robert together. You used to squabble like billy-o.'

'I don't remember that.'

'It's somewhere in the fog of unknowing,' he said. 'That time you can't remember, when you were very small. But the love was always there. You know that, don't you, darling?'

Suddenly, unexpectedly, Phoebe was overcome with tenderness for her frail father, for the times remembered and the times forgotten. She and Robert were in shock, of course, but then so was he. And who was *she* to blame him for anything? She, of all people, whose past was littered with emotional blunders?

'Now, where are those jim-jams?' he said.

Not only jim-jams, but incontinence pants. She left Robert to help him on with these, the ultimate humiliation. Through the door she heard their father trying to make a joke of it. 'Well, my boy, *you* wet your bed until you were four.' Robert said something; her dad laughed.

Once he was ready for bed it was time for his pills. It was fiendishly complicated. Zocor for his heart. Cardizem for his blood pressure. Doxazosin and MiraLAX for goodness knew what. Mandy had sorted them into boxes with little compartments. He swallowed them one by one, as obediently as a child.

'Now I'm afraid it's time for my teeth.'

This was the only time she saw him truly discomforted. More than the incontinence pants. More even than the adultery. She and Robert had forgotten he had dentures. Out they came, with a moist *clunk*. Suddenly he was unsexed and transformed into a crone.

'I'm sorry,' he mumbled, through sunken lips.

'Don't be silly,' said Robert, passing him his glass of

Steradent. Phoebe sensed that these ministrations were softening her brother, too.

Their father's bed was in a small room off the lounge. Robert helped him while Phoebe drew the curtains. Suddenly it hit her – the banality of what they were doing, and yet the vastness of it all.

'God, we haven't even asked what she died from.'

'They think it was an aneurism,' said their father. 'There'll be a post-mortem.'

'Should we be ringing anyone?'

'I think there's an aunt still alive, but she didn't have much family left.' He pulled the duvet up to his chin. 'Only us.'

Upstairs, Robert said he'd sleep in their parents' room. Phoebe took Mandy's. It was even more chaotic than when she'd first glimpsed it – clothes strewn over the unmade bed, a mug of half-drunk tea. A *Mary Celeste* air to it, of somebody who had just stepped out for a moment. She looked at the pegboard of photos, those holiday snaps of Mandy's female friends. Somehow they'd have to track them down and tell them, but it all seemed impossible to contemplate at the moment, along with everything else.

The room had its own washbasin. The shelf was cluttered with the usual assortment of bottles, pots and half-squeezed tubes. Even some mascara and lipstick, though she'd never seen Mandy wearing any. A pot of anti-ageing night cream, whose magical properties might account for her eerie skin. Phoebe washed her face with soap and dried it on Mandy's grubby yellow towel. She hesitated about using her toothbrush but she had no choice, so she squeezed Mandy's toothpaste onto it – Euthymol, something she'd never used. Flinching, she brushed her teeth, leaving an alien taste in her mouth, like wallpaper paste.

Pops. Did Mandy say it as a hint, or did it just slip out?

Phoebe felt dizzy, the past unravelling so fast. Rubbing on the night cream, she looked at the wedding photo. Mandy's mother clung to the arm of a bashful young man with big ears, wearing an ill-fitting suit. She – *Stella* – was no beauty but decidedly voluptuous. Heavy breasts and hips, a body that, like her daughter's, would probably run to fat. She looked fun. Anyone less like Phoebe's mother would be hard to imagine – her gaunt, nervy, classy, beautiful mother, blue-stocking and part-time JP.

She looked around the bedroom. It was as chaotic as a teenager's. No wonder Mandy had made herself at home. It *was* home.

There was a tap at the door and Robert came in, wearing their father's pyjamas. He sat down on the bed.

'Weird, isn't it?' he said.

'Beyond weird.'

Phoebe couldn't wear Mandy's nightie – how could she? She'd stripped to her T-shirt and knickers. Robert shifted over and she climbed into bed. His thick hair was greying; soon it would be as white as their father's.

'I've been thinking about Wales,' Robert said. 'The place we loved. How everything has turned out to be a fiction. Our holidays. My novel.'

'My sort-of-love affair.'

'The words were all lies. Torren's words, our father's words. One big betrayal.'

He rubbed the side of his nose. It was a large nose, like

their father's. The old man's face, however, was looser and more generous. Less handsome than Robert's, certainly, but so very charming.

Robert fingered the crochet flowers of the bedspread. 'I wonder if she made this herself.'

'She had funny taste, didn't she?'

'But she made him happy.'

'They had a hoot.'

Robert nodded. 'If he changed his will, which I suspect he did, she deserved every penny.' He paused. 'God, I'd love a cigarette.'

'She didn't smoke.'

'What's that, then?'

He pointed to an ashtray on the bedside table. They exchanged glances. Phoebe leaned sideways and pulled open the drawer. Inside was a pack of cigarettes and a lighter.

They burst out laughing. So Mandy had another secret up her sleeve. Robert took one and lit up. He inhaled deeply.

For a while they didn't speak. The window was open and the faint sound of a TV drifted in from the cottage next door. It was companionable, their being there together, Phoebe tucked up in bed. They hadn't done it for years, not for all of their so-called adult life. Not since Hafod, where they'd shared a room. Where, at sunset, the bats streamed out of the barn and their parents loved each other.

'What on earth are we going to do about Dad?' he asked. 'I suppose we'll have to start looking for somebody else, but what are we going to do till then?'

'If you'd written *this* as a novel,' Phoebe replied, 'Dad

would die tonight. It would be so beautifully shapely. But life's too messy for that.'

They sat there, wreathed in cigarette smoke, exhausted by the disintegration of their past. They knew life was messy – who didn't, at their age? – but nothing had prepared them for this.

PART TWO

James

When he was a child James liked putting things into boxes. There were owls in the garden of the big house in Hampstead where he grew up, and when he found their pellets he dissected them with a scientist's precision, laid the mouse skulls and beetles' wings in cotton wool, put them in matchboxes and hid them in his bedroom drawer. They joined his other treasures – coins, football cards, scraps of this and that – how thrilling to turn the key and lock them up.

So from an early age he'd learned to compartmentalise.

This was no justification for what happened later. Many years later, when James was a grown man and happened to be attending a conference in Cardiff. He was sitting in the canteen with Hans Tamchina, a colleague from Stuttgart University, who waved his hands around to demonstrate some point and knocked his coffee into James's lap. Luckily it was institutional coffee and therefore tepid, but it was still a shock.

A waitress came to the rescue, carrying a sponge.

'Blimey, it looks like you've—'

'Yes, yes, I know.'

She started giggling, which James thought heartless, and passed him the sponge. 'You'd better do this yourself.'

During the afternoon session the damp patch dried and

at teatime there she was again, the waitress, roaring with laughter at something someone said as she stood behind the urn. After the droning lecture it was a tonic to see her. She fairly crackled with energy. As James joined the shuffling queue she glanced at his crotch and gave him the thumbs up.

He didn't attend the final session. He had a paper to prepare for the following day, so he went outside and sat at a table in the sunshine. It was the university holidays and there were no students around, just a couple of waitresses smoking and talking. One of them was her.

She stubbed out her cigarette and walked over. 'So what do you lot do?'

'We're particle physicists.'

There was a silence.

'Don't worry,' James said. 'Nobody can ever think of anything to say.'

'Except another particle physicist.'

'That's why we need to stick together.'

'You're better behaved than my students, anyway.'

'Clumsier, though.'

Suddenly a gust of wind blew his papers off the table. He jumped up and she helped him collect them.

'It's the wind that's clumsy,' she said.

'Yes, but the wind can't help it.'

'Nor could that bloke.'

She put the papers on the table and weighed them down with the ashtray. He noticed her reddened hands and wedding ring.

'Oh, well,' she said, looking at his scribbles. 'Better let you get on with designing the atom bomb or whatever.'

'I'm afraid somebody else got there first.'

She laughed at this feeble response, the wind blowing the hair across her face. No doubt she was the good-natured sort who would laugh at anything; he felt a small jolt of disappointment.

James watched her as she walked off. Wide hips, heavy-ish legs. Shapely and womanly, in that era of stick-thin girls. There was something bracing about her; she made the air crackle. No doubt it was simply cheerfulness, something that was largely missing from his life at that time.

And he thought no more about it, that August day those many years ago. For he was married, with two small children.

But then she was on the train.

One of his colleagues, a Japanese chap called Itsuki, was helping her lift her suitcase onto the rack.

For a moment, James didn't recognise her. It was start-ling to see her in normal clothes, like a teacher out of school. James was not a visual person, something his wife complained about on the rare occasions she bought a new outfit. But James remembered every detail that day. She wore a sky-blue dress with a wide, buckled belt, and big buttons down the front; she told him later she'd made it herself. On top, a cardigan with little bobbles knitted into it. Her hair was pulled up into a surprisingly formal bun.

She looked genuinely pleased to see him and they sat down opposite each other, in one of those compartments that trains had, in those days. Itsuki must have been sitting in it too, and a couple of other passengers, but he didn't remember them.

'My husband's redecorating the lounge,' she said, 'so I'm leaving him to it. He's ever so finicky, you see, and gets the hump when I just slap it on.' She said she was going up to London to stay with a girlfriend for a couple of days. 'He's painting the flat and we're going to paint the town.'

'Gloss or emulsion?'

'Gloss, of course.' She gazed out of the window at the countryside rattling past. 'I mean, look at this big shiny day!' She turned back to him, her eyes brimming with merriment. 'Three guesses who's going to have the most fun.'

He felt a stab of envy. What a lucky young woman, to feel life vibrating through her like an electrical charge! He thought of a pit pony released into a meadow, tossing its head. Just for a moment he thought of her bun loosening and her hair tumbling down. It was just an idle thought, passing through his mind along with his doubts about the paper he had presented – the reaction had been muted – and whether his car would start. He'd left it at Oxford station and it had been making a rattling noise when he changed gears. As he'd remarked when phoning his wife: 'Cars only make two noises, cheap noises and expensive ones.'

But then he and Stella were talking – he knew her name now. She said her previous job had been at the Imperial Hotel, where she'd learned the silver service. She preferred her present position because she liked being around young people. If she envied the students their education she didn't show it; when it came to class, he would discover, she was without rancour. In fact, it wasn't in her nature to be bitter about anything. He soon found out that she was that rarest of creatures: a happy woman. Something that couldn't be said, with any stretch of the imagination, about his wife.

Fun. That's what they were going to have. Suddenly he envied Stella and her friend, who apparently lived in East Cheam. Like Tony Hancock, he said. Stella loved Tony Hancock so they talked about the blood donor episode, her favourite and indeed his. This led onto the Coronation, how it was the first thing they'd ever watched on TV, and this led onto rabbit-keeping, for some reason, and from there to funny pub names.

'When I was six,' James said, 'the girl next door built a pub in her bedroom, out of a blanket and chairs, and called it The Rosy Arms.' He realised, with surprise, that he'd never told anyone this.

'That is so *sweet*,' she said. 'What did she serve?'

'Liquorice water. Like William Brown.'

She hadn't read the William books so he told her about them. This led on to a disagreement about blancmange – him for, her against. Basically, they nattered. *Babbled,* in fact, which wasn't his sort of thing at all. He wasn't a babbler. He was a talker. But then what did he know? For though he loved Tony Hancock he also loved Montaigne, who understood the fluidity of human nature. *I give my soul now one face, now another, according to which direction I turn it. If I speak of myself in different ways, that is because I look at myself in different ways. All contradictions may be found in me.*

This James, Stella's James, was a babbler. And now he was eating a Kunzle Cake, which Stella had produced from her basket. He licked the cream off his fingers as she uncorked a Thermos of tea. Stella had a sweet tooth; something she would pass on to her daughter. *Their* daughter. Who was unimaginable then, and who would die before he did.

As indeed would Stella. But in 1963 she was a radiant young woman, flushed with high spirits, looking forward to high jinks in London. Buxom, funny, avid for life, not beautiful but utterly gorgeous, with her ruddy cheeks and generous mouth, her earrings jangling as she swung round to point out a field of lapwings, birds which are seldom seen any more.

'Does anyone remember Kunzle Cakes?' James asked Phoebe many years later, sitting there in his tracksuit bottoms. For they, too, had long since gone. Cakes, birds, Stella.

Only he had remained, with memories of that day. A day that changed everything. For he missed his connection at Reading – the 6.15 to Oxford, where his car waited to take him to Summertown, where his wife and children lived – and stayed with Stella on the train, all the way to London.

They didn't sleep together for several weeks. That hardly made him less culpable but he tried to resist, truly he did. He was a married man. Stella was a married woman. Sometimes James felt that their mutual guilt drew them as closely together as their tidal wave of lust.

For that's what it was, in those early weeks. Sitting in the library, the words blurred on the page and became Stella's fingers unbuttoning her blouse and releasing those stupendous breasts. He was stupid with desire. His legs weakened when he stood up to give a lecture. The very sight of a payphone made his heart beat faster.

Finally he surrendered and booked them into the Walnut Tree Hotel in Burford. It was a genteel establishment smelling of floor wax and cabbage, as hotels did then. They signed in as Mr and Mrs Telford, for reasons best known to themselves.

After all the expectation, however, it was something of a let-down. Stella, normally a happy-go-lucky creature, was subdued during dinner and scarcely responded to James's somewhat laboured speculations about their fellow diners. He was sweating with fear – Burford was near Oxford, would someone recognise him? – also with the beginnings of flu.

His condition rapidly worsened and by the time they went to bed he had a raging temperature. Not surprisingly, neither of them had brought a thermometer. Stella helped him into the bath. It was the first time she had seen him naked, and in rather different circumstances than she had imagined – a hunched invalid, petulant and wheezing, his shrunken penis floating in the water, which remained stubbornly lukewarm.

After the bath they did make an attempt at sexual congress but by now his skin was burning and any movement made him nauseous. Though an atheist, he was consumed by a sense of divine retribution. Round and round his fevered brain rolled the words, *The gods make fools of us all*. Stella did her best in her unexpected role of nurse but he flinched at her touch and once actually snapped at her – 'For Christ's sake, woman!' – when she tried to turn him over.

To be frank, he longed to be safely tucked up in his own bed. Illness makes us long for home, and Stella didn't help by telling him about her husband's various ailments, the last thing James wanted to hear. 'He's always had a weak chest, the poor love, he was coughing up his lungs for weeks.' Stella was a glorious woman, but not blessed with tact.

Nor did it help that during that long night, while they lay tossing and turning, James pushing off the blankets and Stella yanking them back, his paroxysms of coughing shaking the bed – nor did it help that through the wall came the thumps and groans of a prolonged copulation that didn't stop until dawn.

It wasn't the best start, if 'best' is an appropriate word to describe an adulterous affair. But, surprisingly enough, this dose of reality plunged them into deeper intimacy and the trysts continued in Burford and various other Cotswolds locations both indoors and outdoors – indeed, sometimes in the very fields in Chipping Norbury with which their daughter would become familiar whilst caring for James in his dotage.

During this time his children simply presumed he was away, because that's what fathers did, and his wife believed he was at one of his conferences – oh, those conferences! Anna was a highly intelligent woman but appeared to suspect nothing. Once the children were born she had given up her career but she had a big, busy life in North Oxford, people in and out of the house all day – neighbours, fellow parents. She cooked the most wonderful dinner parties, organised school events, sat on various boards, worked part time as a JP and created a stunning garden that was opened twice a year in aid of Ugandan lepers. She had a Rolls-Royce of a brain – forensic, dispassionate, scrupulously fair. All in all, she was an admirable woman.

Stella wasn't particularly admirable. Stella was fun. James and his wife had proper conversations about proper things but he and Stella just larked about. Pushing each other off the pavement, snaffling each other's crisps. Just silliness.

Her body; her smell. The laughter at the heart of their lovemaking; the ferocity of their rapture in a hayfield, or in a rented room.

The taste of her.

The jokes evaporated, as jokes do, but he would always remember that.

More months passed. The trees shed their leaves; Christmas came and went. The thing was, he loved them both. Stella wasn't, grubbily, a bit on the side. She filled his heart, which was already full with Anna. They both dwelled there, strangers to each other. Sometimes he felt like a pregnant woman who, unbeknownst to the world, was carrying twins. He never knew that he would be capable of such duplicity, such a slippery accommodation to this dual life in which he found himself enmeshed. And it wasn't as if he was some kind of Lothario. He was a virgin when he met Anna and she and Stella were the only two women with whom he had ever slept.

It was no excuse – no excuse at all – that his was largely a lust-free marriage. He could admit this now. Anna was a highly strung woman who feared losing control. She never flung off her clothes, but folded them before she got into bed. He'd never once seen her on the lavatory. Sometimes he wished she would get roaring drunk and tear off his trousers. It felt like a kind of betrayal, even to admit this to himself. She was so beautiful that the sight of her stopped his heart – olive skin, Aztec cheekbones, something exotic and watchful about her – but she was at her most unreachable when they were making love, which happened only too rarely. What was she thinking, his tense, lovely, complicated wife?

Whereas, as Stella said: 'What you see is what you get.'

How thrilling was this, in its simplicity!

So time passed. James's big, generous, open face was a double-bluff. Like all charmers he made people feel they were the only person in the room. But he had another room beyond that one and maybe more, who knew? He once gave his son a tiny box of drawers with a padlock, because he'd loved squirrelling things away when he was a boy. He called his wife The Sphinx but *he* was the one with the secrets.

A year after he met Stella, he bought Hafod, the holiday cottage in Wales. Robert was eight and Phoebe was six; he bought it so they could run free in the woods and swim in the river and have an old-fashioned childhood.

Curiously enough he didn't mention that ten miles away, near Crickhowell, was a caravan site belonging to a friend of Stella's uncle. A man who apparently turned a blind eye to the comings and goings of its occupants, as long as they paid the rent.

The irony being that for his wife, Hafod was the place she was happiest, because she had him to herself. In fact, it was at Hafod that she shared him. For just ten miles down the hill, in a shabby two-tone caravan with a leaky roof, James lived his other life.

Ken

Ken was a silent man. Of course he talked, when such a thing was necessary, but he was a doer and a fixer. It was his body that spoke. Sturdy, capable Ken, banging in nails and digging up potatoes, holding his wife in his arms at night, keeping the bogeyman at bay. He whistled when he worked. Men did, in those days. In those days, when the two of them were newly married, their world was innocent. He and Stella had known each other since childhood and that glow was still within them, that blithe carelessness that exulted when it rained, when it snowed, when the two of them kicked up the leaves, and in those early months they were carried along in its slipstream. How tender they were with each other, the newest of lovers. And now, wedded.

Ken couldn't believe his luck. Stella was a catch, bees around the honeypot, life and soul of the party. She energised him, she was fun. With her ruddy cheeks, her soft brown hair and wondrous, heavy breasts, she brought him alive. That she was sexually experienced – far more than he was – caused him no pain in those early years. He simply exulted in her. Wordlessly.

He loved her and she loved him. Nothing changed that, through all the troubles that lay ahead. It was a testament to his generosity and to her instinctive, animal tact. Things would change between them, but in those early years they were simply a young couple starting out in life, him up a ladder renovating their home and Stella sallying forth in her uniform and returning, flushed and exhausted, to collapse on the settee and be served a cup of tea by her devoted spouse. They lived in Cardiff, where he worked as a postman, and when dawn broke it was she who brewed up for *him* before crawling back into bed. 'I look out for you,' he said, 'and you look out for me.'

And if she wanted talk there was always her family, the whole nattering crowd of Coxes, living nearby. In those days nobody locked their doors and they were in and out of each other's houses in the street where they lived, long since demolished. They outnumbered Stella's sweet, diffident husband and if he found them raucous and overpowering he kept quiet about that, too. For he had a poor opinion of himself and still marvelled at possessing such a magnificent creature as Stella, with her throaty laugh and dizzying appetite for life.

Besides, he could always escape to his allotment. His shed was his home from home, papered with offcuts and only a feral cat for company. In it, he hammered a crib for their unborn child.

But three years passed and the child didn't arrive.

Stella

Out of sight, out of mind. What you don't know can't hurt you. Stella lived, voraciously, in the present tense. She was a woman of impulse, with strong animal instincts, and to hell with the consequences. This had led her into tricky situations in the past but she'd always been able to block off any unpleasantness, and to blind herself to repercussions. This, the adulterer's most powerful muscle, was one of the few things she had in common with James. This, and an abundance of charm.

For she was loved by the world in general, and most of all by Ken, her kind, sweet husband, with his wide moon face and jug ears – Ken, to whom she ruthlessly blinded herself when she was in the arms of her lover in their draughty, tinny caravan, the rain drumming on the roof, their home from home, their little world, with James reciting her poetry.

> *And now good morrow to our waking souls*, he said,
> *Which watch not one another out of fear;*
> *For love, all love of other sights controls,*
> *And makes one little room an every where.*

Sometimes she couldn't believe that James loved her. He was so distinguished, so awesomely clever. His marriage must be deeply unhappy, she thought. But he seldom spoke of it, and mention of his children plunged him into silence. She was learning how to navigate around him. When it came to men, she wasn't stupid.

And how they larked around! She remembered lying there laughing, her face buried in the pillow, while he ran his finger down her spine. 'You've got one of the six most beautiful backs in Britain.'

'You done a survey then?'

He nodded. 'I have a team in every county.'

'Catch women in butterfly nets, do they? Line them up in an aircraft hangar with a cup of tea and a bun?'

He said that when he was a child he liked collecting things. Butterflies. Owl pellets, filled with bones and beetles' wings. She shuddered at beetles but loved the Beatles and sang him 'Can't Buy Me Love', their latest hit; she knew all the words. He was such a square.

Of course she felt guilty but it was a chronic condition, like her mother's emphysema. And now they had the caravan it was only too easy, horribly easy, to seal themselves off from the world and exist in their own bubble, where they could live their fantasy life, free from responsibility. There was something potent about a caravan, furnished with dolls'-house pots and pans, where they could play at being a couple. And its thrilling air of transience – here today, gone tomorrow, leaving nothing but tyre tracks on the grass. Not that they ever considered running away together, never during those four long years.

The owner turned a blind eye. The two of them felt safe there; they never bumped into anyone they knew. In the holidays the place was so full that they passed unnoticed.

Out of season the caravan park was largely deserted and its few permanent residents singularly lacking in curiosity, being shadowy types who all too visibly had problems of their own. She and James liked making up stories about them. 'Gobby Dobson', who had buried his wife under the patio; 'Bryn Gwyllin-Ap-Gwyllin', who'd been chucked out of the family home for having an affair with a sheep. That sort of nonsense.

It wasn't edifying, any of it. They shouldn't be laughing. They shouldn't be loving each other – heck, he even loved her thick ankles that she'd always hated, even her bunions, the Ugly Sisters of her job. And how carefully they worked on their alibis, the two of them. They were becoming such experts. To the world, James was a vague and amiably bumbling intellectual. In fact, he was a scheming tactician. She herself invented a hotel in Abergavenny where they were frequently short-staffed and called her in as a stop-gap. It was forty miles away – far enough for her to have to spend the night there. This imaginary hotel assumed a weirdly vivid presence in their lives, with its extensive grounds and bossy manager. Sometimes, to amuse themselves, the two of them made up stories about its cast of characters, including a lovelorn bellboy called Dafydd. Sometimes, in fact, it felt as real as the Palisades Holiday Park, Crickhowell, where they actually met.

To be honest, it wasn't the sex. She'd had great sex with a number of men. It was James, however, who discovered her true erogenous zone, her brain. He unstoppered her words that had lain there, dormant, unvoiced throughout her love affairs and marriage to a sweet, silent man who knew so little about her. They gushed forth, and in James's company she opened up like a flower. She was witty, she was clever. She, who had left school at fifteen and never heard of John Donne. It was astonishing to her. It was better than sex. It *was* sex.

That was no excuse. Nothing was an excuse for betraying her beloved husband, who plodded out each morning with his sackful of letters while an hour's drive away she lay in the arms of her bushy-haired professor.

Not *hers*, of course. But hers, just for now.

Sometimes they talked until the birds started singing and the sun rose up behind the Black Mountains. She told him everything, even events in her childhood she didn't remember she remembered. He gave her the words and in return she gave him her body.

In all their conversations, however, she kept one thing to herself. Her deepest sorrow.

James

James was a changed man. A spilled cup of coffee did it. Without that flourish from a German academic he would never have met the second great love of his life.

Outwardly, however, nothing had altered. He disappeared, sometimes for two days at a time. He said he was escaping to Hafod to write. Anna's support of this broke his heart. So did his son's face when James missed his sports day. It wasn't often that he let his children down; he tried, truly he tried, to be there for them, but that caravan had a magnetic pull. Years later, when releasing the newts, James had gazed at the buddleia breaking through the concrete, the sheer force of it, too powerful to resist, and he'd thought of his passion for Stella and her sturdy, intoxicating body.

He knew what people would think: brainy wife versus earthy mistress, lucky bastard; men have been doing it for centuries. Playing away, dipping their wick. Any number of loathsome phrases. Maybe, as Rick said in *Casablanca*, his pitiful excuses didn't amount to a hill of beans in this crazy world. But he was smitten. In Stella's company the grass was greener, the food more delicious even though it was only pasties from the takeaway in Crickhowell. 'Shake, shake the ketchup bottle, none'll come and then a lot'll,' Stella sang as she splashed it over her chips. Her luscious lips, her bitten fingernails, her dirty laugh . . . oh, the delirium of it.

Even in the rain they found ways of amusing themselves. Like many intellectuals, James was mad about ping-pong. Why? God knows. At the Palisades there was a table set up in the Recreation Centre, a corrugated-iron hut next to the toilets, and it was there that he taught Stella to become a demon opponent. Did his children ever cross his mind as he larked around the playground with his mistress, when he should have been playing with them? Indeed, there was a ping-pong table in the barn at Hafod, just ten miles up the road.

In his other life, the one with children in it.

In retrospect the whole thing seemed so unlikely. He, living like a Hobbit in a Welsh caravan park. Trysts in a service station on the M4, Stella still in her waitress uniform. Stolen kisses in the alley behind Chelsea Girl, Cardiff. An existence teetering on a shaky edifice of lies. It was astonishing that he got away with it.

Of course he still loved his wife. As much as ever. Sometimes more. Like every marriage it had its dips and troughs, its moments of soaring joy, its flat periods of contentment. The chemistry constantly changes.

Especially with Anna. His darling, quivery thoroughbred-racehorse of a wife. So volatile, so incandescently intelligent and sometimes – he had to admit it – so difficult. Engaging with her was a thrilling but sometimes exhausting experience. He had nobody with whom to compare her, however. Not until Stella came along, who lived, so simply for the moment. She was the perfect mistress, for she demanded nothing.

An affair, he had discovered, remains aspic'd in the present tense.

Nothing, ostensibly, changed. And four long years passed in a flash. How did they manage to keep it going for all that time, without being discovered? He had no idea. It was so long ago that it felt like a dream. When he was a middle-aged man he went back to Crickhowell, on some pretext or other, and parked outside the Palisades. It was a wet November day and the hills were shrouded in fog. How dank and desolate the place looked now, how exposed their secret! A row of fir trees had been chopped down, to reveal the electricity substation. There were no signs of life, just a couple of crows stepping sideways around the rim of a rubbish bin; stepping fastidiously, as if it were hot. The caravan was still there, smaller and shabbier, dwarfed by a new trailer home topped with a satellite dish.

Our little room an every where. Did he really lie in that caravan spouting John Donne? It was mad, the whole thing was mad . . . the risks they took, the complex logistics and marathon cross-country dashes, the frantic search for a functioning phone box, those Judas coins jangling in their pockets. They were both busy people with full-time jobs; how on earth did they get any work done?

Love is merely a madness; and, I tell you, deserves a dark house and a whip as madmen do; and the reason why they are not so punished and cured is that the lunacy is so ordinary that the whippers are in love too.

It was the ending that jerked them to their senses.

Stella

It was a strain, being the perfect mistress, cheerful and undemanding, even for someone like Stella. She had assumed this role from an early age, as children do in large families. Each settles into a slot, and hers was to be the peacemaker, sunny and emollient, the healer of rifts between her squabbling siblings. Thus was her character set in stone, and it was a struggle to escape that even as an adult. Besides, it was what made her lovable, so why should she stop?

To James she was Little Miss Sunshine, unchanging in her weather. He had enough complications at home. Despite their intimacy, however, he had no idea what was going on in her head and as time passed she was becoming uncharacteristically mutinous. Why should *she* be always at his beck and call, ready to drop everything to rush off and meet him? Was her work really less important than his? She'd already given up her canteen job, which she'd loved, in order to take on temping work, which was more flexible.

And though she gave no sign of it, she burned with a morbid curiosity about his wife and children. Of *course* she did, she was only human. Just occasionally he confided in her – Phoebe in trouble at school, his wife's distress when her mother died – but basically he kept his mouth shut.

They observed the adulterers' pact of silence, the two of them.

She was starting to resent this, however, and to dislike herself for resenting it. Indeed, as time passed, she resented the very fact that James had children at all.

For she and Ken couldn't. It was the sorrow at the heart of their marriage. Several years had passed before he'd finally agreed to a test.

She remembered that day so well, the two of them walking home from the doctor's surgery. There was a heatwave and the tar in the street was melting. They passed the Rec, where naked children splashed in the paddling pool.

'Let's go to the pub,' she said, grabbing his arm.

He shook his head. 'I'm going up the allotment. Radishes won't water themselves.'

Later she found out he'd thrown the crib on a bonfire.

Stella told no one, not even her family. And certainly not James. It would have been an even deeper betrayal of her husband, if that were possible.

But something was changing in her attitude towards him. Didn't he know how lucky he was, having children at all? Yet he took them for granted. Worse than that, he neglected them. He was missing their growing-up, those precious years disappearing in a flash. Their faces emerged from the shadows, a plaintive little boy and girl, the Robert and Phoebe of her imagination. They weren't angry, just bewildered. How could their father be so ruthless?

Yes, Stella could now admit it – ruthless and selfish.

So during that last year she felt herself loosening from

him. The clock was ticking and he was never going to leave his wife. Nor, in fact, was she going to leave Ken. So what were they doing, stuck in a caravan in the middle of a muddy field? They were going nowhere. She gazed at the tyre tracks, and thought: we're getting into a rut, in more ways than one.

His great gift had been his words. But he'd also given her, unwittingly, a vocabulary of discontent. Besides, she was exhausted by the guilt and the lies, by juggling her work and her marriage. She was thirty-one. Her bunions were hurting. Sooner or later she'd have to make a decision.

But then, that final Easter, the decision was taken out of her hands.

James

A little girl disappeared from the caravan site. She was six years old. One minute she was playing in the sandpit next to the shower block, and the next minute she was gone.

Her mother had been distracted by her other child, a baby, yelling its head off in their caravan. It was the first day of the holidays and there weren't many people about – just a few teenagers mooching around the swings and a family unloading their car.

Nobody saw anything. No strange man, no struggle. The little girl had simply vanished off the face of the earth.

The police were called and a huge search was mounted. The national press arrived in droves and the girl's smiling face appeared on all the front pages. The local people rallied round, combing the town and surrounding countryside.

And James was taken in for questioning.

He had been spotted by one of the long-term residents. They said he'd been acting suspiciously, coming and going at odd hours, looking furtive. He had been there that day, with his lady friend, but had left before the alarm was raised. She had left in a separate car.

Somehow, the police tracked him down to his office at the university. The phone rang when he was marking students' papers, and thankfully alone. And then he was driving to Wales in torrential rain, his heart hammering. Anna had no idea where he had gone; he must have gabbled something on the phone. His brain had seized up and he was clammy with sweat. Needless to say he couldn't ring Stella at home. It was a miracle that he didn't crash.

Stella was already at the police station. She stood in the lobby, shaking out her umbrella. For a moment he didn't recognise her; she wore her red PVC raincoat but under the harsh light she looked alien to him. A policewoman touched her arm. She shot James a look – a disconcertingly stern look, like a headmistress – and was ushered away, to be questioned separately.

And then he was sitting in a room that smelled of bleach and cigarettes. A man came in and pulled up a chair. For a moment James thought he was the man who had repaired his car in Banbury, but he introduced himself as Inspector Griffiths. The table between them was empty except for an ashtray full of butts. In those days everybody smoked, whether or not they were being questioned for child abduction.

'You are Professor James Wentworth, of 14 Avenue Road, Summertown, Oxford?'

It was a shock to hear his own address. He realised, then, that Stella didn't even know where he lived.

'Could you tell me your whereabouts on Thursday last week, March 23rd?'

Don't tell my wife.

The inspector took out a notebook and opened it. He sat there, pen poised.

Don't let her know I'm here.

'I was here in Crickhowell, at the Palisades Caravan Park.'

'And why was that, sir?'

'I was visiting a friend.'

'A Mrs Stella Gatterson?'

'Yes.'

'Of 45A, Port Talbot Road, Cardiff?'

'I don't know her address. But I expect that's it.'

The inspector wrote in his notebook. Thin grey hair, the baldness showing through. Footsteps passed in the corridor; somebody laughed.

'Can you tell me the purpose of your visit?' The inspector looked up at him.

'I told you, she was a friend.'

He heaved a sigh. 'How long have you known your friend Mrs Gatterson?'

'About four years.'

'And you've been meeting Mrs Gatterson here, in the caravan park?'

'Yes.'

'You've been driving here, from Oxford?'

'Yes.'

'On a regular basis, would you say?'

James nodded. The inspector raised weary eyebrows.

Love is merely a madness.

It *was* mad. Mad and grubby. This man was getting the picture. To him, James was just another furtive husband, sweating under the harsh strip light.

And now a photo of a smiling little girl was put into his hand. Did he recognise her? No. He didn't see her that day? No.

'Where were you, around half-past four?'

'In the caravan. I imagine.'

There was a silence. The inspector scratched the side of his nose with his pen.

James looked at the photograph of the girl. Pigtails and a wide smile. She was missing a tooth. His own daughter, Phoebe, had recently lost a tooth; he had noticed it only that morning. She told him she'd lost it the week before and had long-ago spent the sixpence.

That's how little he knew of her life.

Suddenly he was overcome with sorrow. For the girl. For being in this barren little room with its yellowing spider plant. For being in that caravan with his wanton mistress and noticing nothing. Why didn't he look out of the window? Lurchingly, he felt that his affair had caused the girl to be stolen away. This was ridiculous, of course. Just as ridiculous as the inspector thinking he was responsible. How could he think that James would harm a child?

But he had. He had harmed his own. It was all his fault, all of it.

As he answered the questions he felt the pressure lifting. The inspector lit a cigarette and James realised that he was no longer a suspect. He had simply become an object of contempt – the weary, indifferent contempt of an officer who had heard it all before so many, many times, in all its tawdry banality.

For that was it, his grand affair. Exposed for what it was, under the brutal strip light, the colour and joy drained from it, revealing the truth. That his thrilling and beloved co-conspirator was simply a pleasant, stout young woman with whom he had nothing in common. Nothing at all.

And that was the end of their relationship. It died that afternoon, in Crickhowell police station, as the two of them sat in their separate rooms telling an officer exactly how, for four years, they'd methodically cheated on their spouses. Their love vanished, just like that. They said good-bye on the steps, with a quick kiss on the cheek, and never saw each other again.

The little girl was never found.

But Stella, the following week, discovered that she was pregnant.

Ken

Stella never came to the allotment; she didn't like mud. On her days off she went window-shopping with her sisters or mooched around Howells department store, fingering handbags and squirting perfumes. Women were mystifying creatures.

Besides, their body clocks were out of kilter, hers and Ken's. She worked late and he left early, ships passing in the night. And now she was taking temporary jobs her hours had become irregular. That she was in such demand was no surprise. He'd seen her serving tables at lightning speed, plates balanced on her arm, that flashing smile and Monroe wriggle. Her effect on men gave him an erotic jolt. It could still catch him by surprise that she appeared to love him.

For Ken had spent their marriage pulled along in her slipstream, her laughter echoing ahead of him. He'd become accustomed to her calling the shots; she was the boss. That he couldn't give her a child was just another reflection of his inadequacy.

He tried not to dwell on this. They never spoke about it.

On his allotment, however, he was a real man. This was his domain, and it was here that he brought life into the world. In his shed the seed potatoes, sitting in their egg boxes, looked almost human, so bald and hopeful. He wanted to plant them with Stella beside him. He wanted to show her off to the other plot-holders, Evan and Dai, Huw and Jock. They had wives who arrived with Thermos flasks and pasties. The men stuffed their produce into their shopping bags; they were respected. Some of the older boys, double-digging their trenches, had even served in the First World War. They had proved themselves to be men – giants among men. On Remembrance Sunday they wore their medals and the crowd saluted.

It was a modest wish, that Stella would come to his plot and admire his handiwork. Ken pictured himself pouring redcurrants into her open palms. He pictured the envy – she was so bloody gorgeous! It was 1967 and hotpants were all the rage. He dreamed of her sashaying down the cinder path and the men dropping their trowels.

There was little likelihood of this, however. Stella showed no interest in his vegetable patch. Besides, she was too exhausted when she came home from work. What ages women spent in the bathroom! He should have got used to it by now but Stella seemed to spend longer and longer in there, doing whatever women did. He'd had no sisters with whom to compare her; she was his first love and he was truly an innocent.

He thought he knew her through and through but nowadays he wasn't so sure. In recent years she had become moodier and less predictable. Altogether trickier. Things between them were changing and he didn't know why. Sometimes she was so very loving. Sitting beside him when he drove, she would cup the nape of his neck in her hand and press her lips against his ear, making him swerve.

'I love you ever so much,' she murmured. 'You know that, sweetheart, don't you?'

This ardour – it was like the early days of their marriage. At other times she was downright irritable. Just recently he'd remarked on the muddy state of their car.

'I told you!' she'd snapped. 'I have to park in the middle of a sodding field!'

'What field?'

'At that place in Abergavenny. The hotel I work at!'

He'd shrunk back, stung.

Nobody had told him this, about marriage. He'd thought that after the first flush of passion things would settle down. How wrong he was. Thomas, his fellow postie, had just gone through a divorce and said he was never going to start on that again.

'Women are like elephants,' he said. 'I like watching 'em, but I don't want to have one.'

Maybe it was pre-menstrual tension. Maybe it was maternal longing that was stirring up the hormones. Truly, Ken hadn't a clue. Lie low, he thought, and keep your mouth shut.

So he was astonished when, one day, Stella appeared at the allotment gates. He'd recognise that red plastic raincoat anywhere. It was a Sunday in late April, the busiest time of year, and he was sowing broad beans. He straightened up and watched his wife approaching. The wind blew a scattering of blossoms around her hair as she passed under the apple tree.

'Thought you'd like some help,' she said, unzipping her coat. Underneath she wore jeans and his old grey sweater, speckled with paint. 'Where do I start?'

Her cheeks were flushed; there was a glow to her. The scruffy clothes made her beauty all the more alluring. Ken had a strong desire to push her into the shed and tear off her clothes. Instead he said: 'You could plant some carrots.' He gave her the packet of seeds. 'Spread apart, not too close. Otherwise they won't fatten up.'

She stayed with him all day. She'd even brought along sandwiches. He didn't tell her what a pleasure it was because this would make them both awkward. Instead, he gave her instructions and watched her inching along on her knees, sprinkling seeds fastidiously between finger and thumb as if she were sprinkling salt on her dinner. She was doing it too thickly but he didn't stop her. The sun came out and she sat back on her haunches, pushing her hair off her face and leaving a smear of mud on her cheek.

How he loved her that day! All of a sudden she was the supportive wife. He had no idea what caused it, but something had changed her.

Back home this mood continued. She no longer seemed distracted. Quite the opposite, in fact; she seemed to be devoting herself to him and tenderly anticipating his needs. She rose at dawn to make his tea, something she hadn't done for years. To his astonishment, she even darned his socks. Their rolled-up balls, laid on the bed, brought tears to his eyes.

And then, at the beginning of May, he learned the reason for this shift in temperature. She told him she was pregnant.

Kenneth would live for another forty years. As time passed he dwelled more and more on the past, and thought a great deal about this seismic period.

For it was, indeed, seismic – catastrophic, surely. His

wife had been having an affair for four long years and was now carrying another man's child. She said the man had no idea she was pregnant and that the affair was over. She tried to tell Ken the details but he didn't want to hear.

He remembered it so clearly. Stella standing at the kitchen sink, a sponge clutched in her hand.

'I'm so sorry,' she said. 'I'm so, so sorry.'

Through the window, the sunlight caught the back wall of their yard. He noticed an elder shoot pushing its way through a crack in the brickwork. *I'd better get rid of that before it pulls the wall apart.*

Odd how he could think this at the very same time as his life unravelled. What was odder, however, was his reaction to her words. Of course he felt betrayed and deeply, deeply hurt. But he didn't feel angry.

Maybe he'd always felt so inferior that it was understandable, her falling in love with somebody else. Maybe he was just weak. Maybe the news of her pregnancy blotted it out.

She sat down heavily on the stool. For a while they didn't speak. She took his hand.

'I don't expect you to forgive me, love.' She stroked his fingers one by one, considering them, her head tilted. 'I'll leave if you want me to. You've got every right to chuck me out.'

'Don't go!' He jerked her head up. 'That would be daft.'

They gazed into each other's eyes. Outside, the ice-cream van started playing. It was teatime and the children would be coming out of school.

But the two of them were oblivious. It was just him and her, alone in the world, her face tilted up to him.

'Does anyone know about this baby?'

She shook her head.

He moved away from her and leaned against the fridge. He felt a surge of power. She was totally his. Strange timing, after what he'd just heard, but this was how he felt.

'Don't tell them.'

Later they went swimming in the local baths, something they hadn't done for years. Stella was a powerful swimmer – she'd been the school champion – and matched him stroke for stroke. Afterwards they sat on the edge of the pool, panting. She pulled off her cap and shook her hair free. They sat there in silence, swinging their legs in unison. Ken stole a look at his wife's belly. Was it his imagination, or was it fatter? In her sleek black swimsuit she was a new creature to him, a seal-wife, a creature of the deep, with a new creature inside her. He still couldn't comprehend the enormity of it.

'I burnt the crib,' he said, but she didn't hear. She was jabbing her finger into her ear, to unblock it.

They called in sick and took the next day off. They stayed indoors with the curtains closed, and didn't answer the phone. And all day they talked. Frankly, truthfully; it seemed for the very first time. He never knew he had so many words in him.

'I hear you laughing with your girlfriends,' he said, 'and I think: you never laugh like that with me.'

'That's because they're women, silly. We have more fun than men.'

He was Mr Safe and Steady. He didn't mind, he said, he loved looking after her, but sometimes she took him for granted. He said it hurt him that she never wore the mauve sweater he gave her. He talked about his sense of failure for not giving her a child. Oh, it all came out as he sat there holding her hand. Once or twice, tears filled her eyes when his words hit home. They never mentioned her lover; he seemed strangely irrelevant, now. The outside world, too, seemed very far away. It was just the two of them, opening up to each other for the very first time.

At lunchtime she fried them eggs, his browned on both sides, the way he liked them, and hers soft, the yolk spilling out. They were very close, that day. It grew chillier and they wrapped themselves in blankets, like a pair of invalids. And still they talked.

Outside they heard the voices of children in the street. The van played its siren tune. A whole day seemed to have been and gone.

He went into the kitchen to make them a cup of tea. As he filled the kettle it truly hit him. Maybe it was delayed shock.

His wife was pregnant.

What a catastrophe. And yet not a catastrophe at all. A sheer, dizzying joy.

The realisation made him breathless. It was at this moment, pausing at the tea caddy, that he made up his mind. He carried in the mugs and eased himself down beside her. When he spoke, it was with a new, manly confidence. For the first time, he was in charge.

'We're going to keep this baby,' he said, 'and bring it up as our own.'

She stiffened beside him, not daring to breathe.

He put his finger to his lips, *sssh,* and whispered: 'Mum's the word.'

'Mum?' she said, and suddenly burst out laughing. 'It's that all right.'

So began a whole new period in their marriage. Sometimes Ken thought that their previous life had just been a rehearsal – an affectionate but rudimentary thing based on goodwill, bodily comfort and humdrum daily doings. And something further in the past – pelting each other with snowballs, kicking up leaves, their shared youthful exuberance. Now it had deepened; now that they had both spoken frankly, their life together was truly beginning.

His own generosity had surprised him. He had taken on another man's child without a word of recrimination. Stella's gratitude at his tolerance had shifted things between them. His brazen wife had become meeker and more compliant. More loving. Before, he'd felt somewhat peripheral, the mute partner in their marriage; the way she lit up in company had hurt his feelings. This vanished; he was the centre of her life now, he had her to himself. It was the two of them against the world, bonded together with their huge and thrilling secret.

For they told nobody the truth. Even Stella's sisters, with whom she was close. Her family simply celebrated the happy announcement. Ken's workmates took him to the pub and got him drunk. It was 1967 and the Summer of Love, even in Cardiff. People were stripping off and dancing in the streets; the old certainties were being torn up and thrown to the wind. Ken's subversive act of rebellion seemed to have infected the country.

And the wonder was that he soon believed in his own lie. He thought of the true father less and less. The man's name had scarcely been mentioned; Ken knew nothing about him and didn't want to know. Just occasionally he was brought up short. Once, for instance, when Stella tactlessly laughed: 'I hope it has my looks and his brains, not the other way round.'

But he was steadily laying claim to his future child, discussing names with his wife, buying her vitamins and accompanying her to the ante-natal clinic. The other man was fading away; *this* was the reality.

'*This*,' he said, stroking Stella's belly.

The miracle of it had become his miracle too. He was proud of himself, of his own largeness of heart. It had taken him by surprise but now they were settling into their new roles, the two of them. In fact he sometimes felt grateful to this unknown man for bringing them closer.

During that summer the country sweltered in a heat-wave. As he sweated on his rounds, Ken considered the future. An idea was brewing – more than an idea, a profound urge that gathered its own momentum. Back at the depot he looked at his mates. He liked them well enough but if he never saw them again he'd not miss them.

Stella was working at the Royal Hotel, down by the docks. When she came home she sat slumped on the settee, fanning herself with the gas bill. Ken brought her a Lucozade and sat down beside her.

'I've been thinking, love,' he said. 'What would you say to moving out of Cardiff? Going somewhere else and making a fresh start, just the two of us?'

She put down the glass and stared at him. 'You mad? I'm having a baby in November.'

'The three of us, then.'

'Move *away*? But what about my family?'

I want you to myself. He didn't say this, of course.

'I'm having a baby; I'll need them more than ever,' she said. 'Anyway I'd miss them, I love them. It's all right for you, you haven't got anyone except me.'

There was a silence. He could hear her breathing heavily. Taking her hand, he said: 'We wouldn't be moving to Timbuctoo. You'd still see your family. I just think we should go someplace where nobody knows us. Where nobody knows what's happened, and there's no chance they'd find out. I think it would lift a big weight off our minds. It's going to haunt us otherwise – we'll always be on our guard. This way we can put it behind us and move on.' He paused. 'It's not as if we're even Welsh.'

She burst out laughing. 'That's the least of it, sweetheart.' She put her finger on his chin. 'You're a caution, you are.'

Over the next few days, however, he could see her softening. After all, she was deeply in his debt and in no position to argue. Besides, her favourite sister, Corinne, had already moved to London. Why should she, Stella, stay stuck in a back street in Cardiff, kept awake by the drunken brawling of the new couple who'd just moved in upstairs?

His wife had always been up for adventure; he'd had plenty of proof of *that*. By the end of the week he knew he'd won, when she said: 'So what are we going to do then, stick a pin in the map?'

It wasn't quite such a gamble, but close. The brother of a fellow postie was moving out of his flat in Solihull, where he had a full-sized allotment complete with fruit bushes, a pear tree and a large, brand-new shed.

That decided it. Ken, usually so cautious, such a plodder,

had revealed himself to be as reckless as his wife. So the two of them moved to Solihull. He got a job with the Royal Mail and she gave birth to a baby girl. They called her Amanda. It was not his choice, this name, but marriage was a question of give and take, wasn't it? He'd learned a lot, these past few months.

And with her birth he'd joined the world of men. He was a father, and their new life could begin.

Mandy grew up to be a sturdy, cheerful little girl, the image of her mother. If there was a trace of someone else there, Ken chose to ignore it. Some people even saw a resemblance to himself, surprisingly enough, saying she had his nose. He loved the child with a ferocity that took him by surprise. How protective he felt! It was as if his own skin were flayed, exposed to the terrors and joys of the world on her behalf. *The price of love is pain.* He'd laid claim to his daughter the moment he forgave his wife and welcomed her into the world. And he'd earned her love by being her father, through the years of sleepless nights and nappy changes, of chicken pox and interminable hours of pushing her on the swings in a freezing playground. Years later, when she was a middle-aged woman, Mandy told James: 'My dad was always there for me.' Words that made the old man wince.

Time passed. Mandy started primary school. Her mother, larger now but perennially ebullient, stayed at home to look after her. And in his shed, his home from home, Kenneth built his daughter a dolls' house. Four rooms, a staircase, tiny items of furniture. It was Mandy's own home from home, where she could live another life and make up her own stories. *Our little rooms an every where.*

PART THREE

Phoebe

'I can see what Dad meant, about caravans,' said Robert, who was now living in one. 'Every day's a holiday and you've got everything you need. All that *stuff* we had, the endless, endless stuff in that stonking great house. You buy stuff you don't need with money you don't have, and all you're doing is wrecking the planet and feeding the big corporations, and does it make you happy? Does it hell.'

'Excellent,' said Phoebe. 'You're becoming a true Knocktonian.'

This was not surprising as Robert was now living in her town. His caravan was in an orchard next to the recycling centre, out beyond the bypass. He'd moved into it to consider his options while the house in Wimbledon was being sold. It had been a year now, however, and he seemed quite content. He said he felt as free in his caravan as he'd felt in his shed. Freer, in fact, because his marriage had been lifted off him.

In the evenings he watched his tiny TV. One day, he said, he might switch it on, see Farida and think: good God, I was married to her once.

The thought of Torren, in retrospect, seemed even more unlikely. He'd left the area some months earlier. Phoebe had heard the news from her neighbour Abbie, who was in the Memorial Hall car park nailing up a sign for her Weight Loss Support Group. By the way she casually brought up the subject, Phoebe realised that she had been one of Torren's conquests and suspected that she, Phoebe, had been one too. 'Gone, just like that,' Abbie said. 'But then he'd always been a free spirit.' By the dreamy look in her eyes, Phoebe could tell she knew nothing about Croydon, and she didn't disabuse her.

A few days later she drove into Torren's wood. She passed the rusting motorbike entrails, smothered in brambles. The totem pole, now leaning at an angle. She drove down the track and parked in the clearing. Tyre tracks were scored in the grass and the door of his hut hung open. Either he'd left in a hurry or couldn't be bothered to close it, because there was nothing worth stealing.

Inside it was the usual mess. It looked as if he'd just stepped out for a moment; he seemed to have taken nothing with him. So much stuff, as Robert would say, even for someone living the simple life.

Phoebe sat on the bed, its springs creaking, and looked around for one last time. Soon nature would reclaim Torren's rural shagpad where once she'd spun her fantasy life. On the wall, his Pink Floyd poster had loosened from the wall and lolled like a tongue. A bird must have been nesting in the ceiling because broken eggshells lay on the floor, and a smear of yolk. She wondered if she would ever have sex again.

Before she left, she went down to the stream. Maybe, at last, she would see that otter. But all she found was a freshly dug grave and a wooden cross saying *Ziggy*.

Robert

Robert had erected a yurt in the orchard for when his children came to stay. It was never too late to get the hippie vibe. Unlike his sister he'd missed it the first time round. He had been a conventional youth and anxious to please his parents, but now he was of mature years this hairy, earthy lifestyle, waking up to birdsong and digging his vegetable patch, filled him with contentment. He'd even enrolled in a Yin Yoga class with somebody called Philomena Hodge. His old world was a world away, and what a messy, corrupt and distracting world that was! He didn't watch the news. Farida's crimson lips no longer distracted him. Terrorists came and went, so did ghastly American presidents and mad dictators with even madder hairstyles.

People who live in the country had always known this. The earth turned with the seasons and there was always planting to be done. Who cared if it rained? There was no such thing as bad weather, just the wrong clothes. Robert whistled as he strode through the mud and flung branches onto the bonfire. Soon he would get a dog. Heaven knew why he gave his Radnorshire chaps such a hard time.

It still made him blush to think about his novel. When his sister was young she used to play the guitar and sing 'I Ain't Got Nothin' but the Blues' in her piping middle-class voice. She even wore a *harmonica harness*, for fuck's sake.

When he wanted to mortify her he brought this up. However, he too had his humiliations. Thank God his sister hadn't read his book; he'd never have lived it down.

And now he was 6,000 words into his second *opus*. Who said that writing a novel was like banging your head against your computer until your forehead bled? But he had to persevere, just to restore some self-respect. The world didn't need another book but when did that stop anybody? And this time the subject was closer to home.

It was called *Vaguely With Lorna* and it told the story of Buffy's ex, the woman who put newts into a pond to stop a bypass being built. When speaking her name, Buffy's voice became golden syrup'd with love. He was an old ham, of course, from his days on the stage. But he did seem to be on excellent terms with most of his exes. Robert considered this the mark of a stylish man and had followed his example in his dealings with Farida.

To be frank, his wife had made this easier by admitting she'd been having an affair. This emerged when he told her he wanted a divorce. The bloke was half her age, a grip at the TV studios, and it had been going on for a year.

'You really think I didn't know?' he'd said. That was a lie, of course; he hadn't the faintest idea. It was gratifying, however, to see the confusion on her face. Between the two of them, he could feel that familiar tidal pull – just for a moment, he was the winner.

It hadn't been a pleasant sensation. His heart seemed to be swallowing itself, a lurch deep in his chest. He and Farida had been sitting in an Uber, on their way to a party in Clerkenwell. Tears sprang to his eyes – shameful tears. He lowered his head and gazed at her satin cargo pants.

Oh, waist down I just wear my knickers. He remembered Mandy's incomprehension; how he and Farida exchanged glances. The Uber passed some smokers, huddled outside a pub and laughing soundlessly. Their own jokes, his and Farida's, had long since drained away; they were the first thing to go when a marriage was dying. Now it was truly dead; Farida's words had given it the knock-out punch. He hadn't seen those cargo pants before, with their useless satin pockets halfway down the thigh. They must have been new. From now on, his wife would be buying clothes with which he'd be unfamiliar.

He couldn't start thinking about that sort of thing. He had to concentrate on the here and now. A party to get through, with this disappeared woman at his side. The yawning chasm of the years ahead.

But he couldn't get his brain to engage. Since, drunkenly in their kitchen, he'd brought up the subject of divorce, events had gathered their own momentum and slipped out of his control. Tonight a new person had popped up, Ivan. Of course he'd be called Ivan. Ivan the grip – what the hell did grips do?

The weird thing was that, despite his distress, Robert had felt only the mildest jealousy. Instead, he'd felt a sick lurch of superiority – a feeling so rare it had taken him by surprise. The party was held in a cavernous loft – the obligatory brick walls; kitchen units salvaged from a butcher's shop. Though bleached and scrubbed, the wood was soaked in the blood of blameless cows, thousands of them. How thin was the veneer of good behaviour! He'd gazed at the guests, knocking back the Bellinis. QCs, captains of industry. They were Farida's friends, not his, but for once she didn't mingle. She'd stood at his side like a faithful wife, foraging, with her painted nails, into a tiny cone of fish and chips. The two of them chatted about politics, her voice over-bright. He found this strangely touching.

And her guilt did ease the weeks that followed. She didn't do dote – it didn't go that far – but she became gratifyingly solicitous, sometimes downright humble. *Humble.*

In fact, the death of their marriage brought them closer than they'd been for years. They crept shakily around the house nursing cups of strong sweet tea, as if they'd been in an accident, and stayed up late, talking. Amongst the revelations, he told her he'd never liked their house. He could admit it now. 'It's got no past,' he said, 'no memories.' The children weren't brought up there, it was like living in a show home. A nowhere place, all polished steel and digital control panels pulsing and bleeping – God knew what they all did. 'To be honest,' he said, 'I was happier in my shed.'

To their parents' mortification, Jack and Alice said they'd seen it coming for years. They rallied round the two of them, helping them pack up their marriage like the most understanding of removal men. And throughout it all Farida behaved remarkably well. Like Edward Heath, she was at her best when leaving office.

Since then Phoebe's friend Buffy had become Robert's confidant. Buffy was something of an expert in these matters. Towards only one of his exes did he bear any ill will. She was called Jacquetta and was apparently one of those vague, arty women who were two a penny in Knockton. The moment she and Buffy split up, however, the vagueness vanished and she hired a red-hot lawyer who screwed everything out of him, even his beloved Ivon Hitchens painting, a cause of bitterness to this day.

Robert saw a lot of Buffy because his father had moved into his hotel. The old man lived in an annexe overlooking the garden, with a carer visiting twice a day.

In truth, he should have been in a proper Home, but they were all in denial about this. The very word 'Home' spelled finality whereas, as his father said, the word 'hotel' was full of possibilities. He sat in the lounge nattering to Buffy and Monica. He drank martinis and talked to the other guests. Sometimes Phoebe or Robert wheeled him down the High Street to have lunch in Angie's Bistro. He was a lucky old sod – what had he done to deserve it? But then he'd been lucky all his life. And who said that life was fair?

Robert, recovering from his own *Sturm und Drang*, had grown more tolerant of his father. Over the past few months the dad-ness had disappeared and the man was revealed – charming all right, but pretty spoilt and self-absorbed. In fact, downright ruthless, as they had discovered. A man highly intelligent when it came to his incomprehensible work, but less so when emotions were involved. An absent father but, what the hell, the man had been in love. In other words, just a normal, faulty human being, like everyone Robert had ever known. Like, of course, himself.

Phoebe, however, was still angry with their father. She was sixty-one now and should have got over it. When Robert told her this, however, she snapped at him: 'It's all right for you, you're a bloke.'

What was *that* supposed to mean? Were they really regressing to that old *Men-are-from-Mars* stuff? He'd thought that the two of them had forgotten their old squabbles and drawn together, but she flared up when he tried to defend their father.

Maybe she felt invaded, with the two of them moving into her town. Robert couldn't remember who'd suggested it but it seemed an ideal solution for them all. Wasn't that what families were supposed to do? Pull together, support each other? Farida's words had hit home.

And he'd been trying to respect his sister's privacy. He always phoned before he visited. He hadn't joined her choir even though they were desperate for a baritone. He didn't want to encroach. He wasn't an insensitive chap. He was a *writer*, for Christ's sake.

Then suddenly the clouds would open and peace was restored. Robert was used to this. He'd lived with Farida for thirty-five years, he should have got the hang of women by now. Phoebe would tramp across the orchard with a bottle of Rioja and they'd sprawl together on his midget sofa and watch his midget TV. God, he loved her. She would tell him the local gossip. How a woman called Lulu Baines, who ran the Knockton Bat-Watching Club, was having an affair with a man she found drunk in a skip. Someone had discovered a donkey in their living room. That sort of thing. All good material for his novel.

'And they gossip about you,' said Phoebe. 'A mysterious man in a caravan.'

'I thought there're loads of them around here.'

'They're not as clean as you.' She looked at him, her head tilted. 'Anyway, some of the women are desperate.'

They laughed. Phoebe looked at the plywood walls. 'Are you sure you can stick another winter in this ghastly place? There's no insulation.'

'I'm as snug as a bug in a rug.' He shrugged. 'If it was good enough for Dad, it's good enough for me.'

'But he had his mistress to keep him warm.' She looked out of the window. In the gathering dusk, apples lay scattered under the trees. 'I think we should go there.'

'Go where?'

'To Crickhowell. To the caravan park.'

He stared at her. 'Why?'

'My therapist says I need closure.' She raised her eyebrows. 'Anyway, I'm curious.'

Robert told himself it was just a jaunt. That was how Mandy would have described it, if she were still alive.

In a strange way, however, she *was* still with them. This was the place where she came into the world, and another little girl disappeared from it. It seemed too momentous for somewhere as humdrum as a caravan site. Toilet block, clock golf. Tupperware. That sort of thing. Maybe a row of those dispiriting leylandii to act as a windbreak against the howling Welsh gales. Anything less conducive to a love affair would be hard to imagine.

Robert had pictured it so often that it had assumed its own reality. His father had told them nothing except, for some reason, its proximity to a row of abandoned garages. Maybe he was trying to defuse the romance of the place. If so, it had the opposite effect. Surely it was a tribute to their passion that it could flourish in such depressing surroundings.

At first Robert resisted the idea of going there. The thought of his father's other life made his stomach churn. He was feeling stir-crazy, however, in his own particular caravan, and wanted to support his sister. It was a beautiful autumn day and he'd never been to Crickhowell, though it was only ten miles from Hafod. On holiday he and Phoebe just mucked about in the woods.

So they drove there and discovered a market town very like Knockton – farmers and beardies, arty women looking like Phoebe, elderly ramblers. There was no sign of a caravan park and the couple of people they asked had never heard of one.

The butcher's, however, had a sign saying it was established in 1920 so that looked promising. They went in and asked the man behind the counter. He wore a bloodstained apron and looked encouragingly ancient. He pointed them in the right direction but said the park had long since gone.

In his heart of hearts Robert had suspected this. In fact it was something of a relief. Now they'd arrived, however, they decided to walk there.

It wasn't far. They passed the electricity substation and a row of garages. A few yards down the road they stopped. Ahead of them stood a row of flagpoles and a sign: *The Palisades: 80% Sold.*

It was a development of starter homes. The two of them wandered aimlessly down a cul-de-sac. Each garden was surrounded by close-board fencing. Children's voices could be heard on the other side. Behind one fence there must have been a trampoline because, above it, a little girl's head rose and fell. She had bright red hair; it floated up and down, up and down, fiery in the setting sun.

For some reason Robert and Phoebe were seized with high spirits and sang all the way home. They used to sing in the car when they were little. They sang 'Fatty Bum Bum'. Then

Phoebe sang the Tom Paxton love song that she used to play on her guitar, 'The Last Thing on my Mind'. Over the years her voice had slipped from soprano to a cracked alto.

When they arrived back in Knockton they saw an ambulance parked outside the Myrtle House Hotel. This time they wouldn't be fooled. It would be one of the guests who'd broken their leg tramping along Offa's Dyke. The path ran through the woods nearby, sinking into ditches gnarled with roots and then up onto the hills where it was studded with rocks.

But they were wrong, of course. The ambulance was for their father.

After the funeral they sorted through their father's stuff. Their mother used to organise his filing system, but since her death it had descended into chaos. Nowadays the bulk of his paperwork was filed under *M* for *Miscellaneous*. His will was there – he had indeed left some money to Mandy. His pension documents and modest investments were all stuffed into that bulging file.

Phoebe was sorting them into piles when she found a letter.

It was from their mother, to their father.

Anna

To be opened after my death.

Dearest love,

Death does solve those difficult conversations, doesn't it? Rather a radical solution, I grant you, but we all have our secrets. You had yours and I had mine. The difference is that I knew yours from the very beginning, whereas mine has been locked away in my heart for many years, from a time long before you came into my life, bicycling down Clarendon Street, laughing like a hyena, with your gown billowing behind you.

I fell in love with you straight away. You were so brilliant and charming and you oxygenated my brain. God, you made me happy. Life came so easily to you, whereas for me it's always been a struggle, you know that better than anyone, but your love transformed my life, and so we started on our long adventure. First, the bedsitter in Green Street, the lorries trundling past, and Oxford's nosiest landlady downstairs, but what did we care? How we laughed and how we talked, the words spilling out, the lilac tree outside our window frothing into blossom, spag bol for supper and your arms around me every night. And how hard we worked, sitting at opposite ends of the table with our papers spread out in front of us. When you looked up, there I was, and when I looked up, there you were, just like Gabriel Oak. We were going to do such great things in the world.

But our little idyll was over in a flash, because along came the babies and bang went my career. You never really understood what that meant to me, did you? In those days it was the norm that women looked after the children. You had no idea what it was like, the grinding boredom, the atrophied brain, the mind-numbing domesticity, the count-down till bedtime. Every day, like millions of men all over the country, you did your disappearing act. I saw the spring in your step when you closed the front door.

To be perfectly frank, they weren't the easiest children to love. I tried to, truly I did. But Robert was such a whiney little boy. Moan, moan. He could even grumble while sucking at my nipple. And Phoebe was so difficult. Not with you – oh, both of them were so sweet with you, they worshipped you, the absent father who swooped into their life when he felt like it and spoiled them rotten – something I had to rectify, much to their resentment, when you'd disappeared back into your career. It's no fun being the bad cop.

I thought we'd produce two prodigies but no luck in that department either. We never mentioned it, did we? But neither of them was as clever as you. Or, to be per-fectly frank, me. It didn't help that Robert was so lazy, and Phoebe was so contrary.

You let them get away with it because your mind was elsewhere. Up in the rarified air of higher physics. And down and dirty with Stella.

Of course I knew. I knew straight away. Men are such

chumps – even men with Double Firsts. Especially men with Double Firsts. You became more attentive and yet more distracted. You started giving me too much informa- tion about where you were going, and I hadn't even asked. The coins jangling in your pocket when you went for a 'walk' to the telephone box round the corner. All the tell- tale signs. It was so corny, so demeaning, for you as well as for me. We'd given our hearts to each other, we had something so rare and wonderful, and suddenly you were simply a furtive adulterer with lipstick on your collar. You, my darling James, of all people.

At first I was angry. How could you do this to me when I was at my lowest ebb? Run ragged with two children and elbow-deep in dirty dishes? Trying to cope in a draughty house with a leaking roof and all those rooms to clean? But I kept quiet, coward that I was, because I was terrified of losing you. If I put it into words it would all come out into the open and you'd have to make a choice. So I shut up and hoped the whole thing would blow over.

When we bought Hafod I really thought it had. For over a year while you'd been leading a shadowy parallel life, I'd felt it like the rumblings of the Underground beneath our feet and in a strange way I'd got used to its rhythms – your periods of exhilaration and tristesse, your sudden impul- sive hugs, as if thanking me for my ignorance. I really thought it had run its course and you wanted to make a fresh start.

How stupid I was. How very stupid. Keats fled to Italy to escape his TB. Can you imagine how he felt when he still coughed up blood in his handkerchief? That's how I felt when your symptoms continued in Wales. Still I kept quiet, and you suspected nothing. We each had our secret and in a strange way I felt complicit in your clumsy excuses and alibis.

I still had no idea who the woman was. I didn't demean myself by searching your pockets. But I knew she was giving you something that I never could.

But I don't need to spell this out. Believe me, your tenderness and consideration over the years is something for which I've always been grateful. In every other way we have been so marvellously compatible, haven't we? I do believe we've had a marriage of true minds. We've never stopped talking, we find each other endlessly interesting, we respect each other's opinions even when violently disagreeing. Living with you has been the most exhilarating experience, and my heart has always been yours.

So I let you get away with it. As time passed I watched you grow more confident. If it wasn't so painful it would have been funny; remember when the children were young and they played hide-and-seek by hiding in FRONT of a tree? You thought you were being so careful but you kept slipping up. I remember Tim phoning, from your department, when you'd told me that the two of you were at a symposium in Norwich. What rankled was that I found myself lying on YOUR behalf. Which was a touch ironic, wasn't it?

Another annoying thing was the way you took the car at Hafod, and left us alone there. Have you any idea what it was like to be stuck with the children all day, and then find we'd run out of bread? I did put my foot down about that, so you started taking taxis.

By then I knew where you were going. Do you remember

that 'lecture in Leeds' you were supposedly giving? You told me in some detail about taking the car to Abergavenny station and the train from there. When you returned, the next day, I found a receipt in the back seat, from an off-licence in Crickhowell.

For a while I did nothing. The thought of nosing around our local town made ME feel like the transgressor, rather than you. But something cracked when you broke your promise to take the children to that llama farm, do you remember? They'd looked forward to that outing for days. Their reaction broke my heart, for this time they'd grown so used to it they didn't even cry.

Our poor children. I tried to be a good mother but it didn't come naturally. It was you they loved with a passion. How jealously they fought for your attention! Because you were indeed a marvellous father, I've already told you that – warm and funny and never patronising, treating them as equals, interested in what they were doing, suddenly gathering them into your arms with great bellows of joy. My only consolation is that they've never had their illusions shattered. For they've never known, and never will know, about you and Stella.

Oh, yes, I found out her name. Stella Gatterson. It was soon after the llama incident. I went to the taxi firm in Crickhowell and said you'd left your wallet in one of the cabs. That's how I discovered where you'd been going for your little trysts. They found the driver who'd taken you to a place called the Palisades Holiday Park, out on the Brecon road. He even took me there, as he was going that way, and pointed out your particular caravan.

Do you know, I burst out laughing? I'd imagined a

discreet little hotel. I simply couldn't picture you there in that shabby tin box, parked between the toilets and the sandpit. It was out of season and the place was deserted. God knows why it was called the Palisades when it was smack up against a row of garages and an electrical substation. I thought of our large, comfortable home in Oxford with its beautiful garden. I thought of our seventeenth-century farmhouse with its inglenook fireplace and barn owls and view of the Black Mountains.

I wasn't laughing now. My God, you must have loved that woman.

I found out her name from a boy in the office. He was lying on the floor reading the Beano. His dad ran the caravan site but he was apparently out, which was fortunate, because my enquiry might have seemed odd. The boy liked Stella because she played clock golf with him and let him win.

I drove home to Oxford, numb with shock. My insides had turned to water. At one point I pulled off the road and plunged into some bushes where I had violent diarrhoea. I wished to God I hadn't seen that caravan. It made it all so horribly real.

You were away in Singapore at the time. When you returned you suspected nothing. I behaved as usual and the weeks passed. But now I had a location my brain was poisoned with images. You were hurrying down the cinder path, looking around furtively, tapping on the caravan door and disappearing inside. I glimpsed Stella in the window, her face blurred. I saw you pulling down the blind. I saw children playing innocently outside – did you hear their voices and feel a stab of guilt? I saw the caravan vibrating, like some ghastly cartoon.

I'm sure you met in other places, but that holiday park stuck in my mind. Obsessively, I made up scenarios. Some were so lurid they make me blush, even now, but funnily enough it was the humdrum ones which affected me the most. The two of you playing at clock golf, and washing up in a little plastic bowl. Bringing back bottles from the off-licence – Guinness for you, but what for Stella? She altered all the time, you see. Sometimes I pictured her blonde and blowsy, a Benny Hill kind of girl – she'd drink Babycham. Sometimes she was coltish, with auburn curls and a mini-skirt, swigging Coca-Cola. Then there was a Juliette Gréco-type, black eyeliner and polo-neck, and she'd be drinking absinthe and smoking a Sobranie. This last Stella was the least convincing but then she could be a middle-class girl who was slumming it. After all, YOU were slumming it. And what's infuriating is that you'd always sneered at caravans, you thought them suburban and swore at them when they hogged the road.

Both our children liked making up stories, didn't they? Robert's in particular were pretty creative, which is unusual in a boy. But strong imaginations can be a curse. Over those weeks I could feel it eating away at me, like the cancer is consuming me now.

I lost weight, I couldn't eat. It was so long ago I'm sure you don't remember. I wished to God I hadn't made that trip. Of course I knew something was going on but the proof took on a life of its own. Stella was growing so vivid in my imagination, so poisonously vivid, that for my own survival I had to lance the boil. I had to meet her.

So I did.

Ha! That's stopped you in your tracks, hasn't it? I

wonder where you're reading this? I'm picturing you at Rose Cottage, sitting on our love-seat, which celebrated our long and happy marriage. Which it has been, my darling. Happy beyond words. We talked about everything in our long conversation – everything but this. And we were so young that it feels a lifetime away; that was in another country, and besides the wench is dead. Indeed, Stella could be, by now. But even today I can remember my heart hammering as I dialled her number.

The boy had told me she lived in Cardiff, you see. With that surname it was easy. I rang Directory Enquiries who told me there was only one Gatterson and gave me the information.

In those quaint days we only had that one phone, in the living room, so I waited until you were at work and the children at school. It was a dank day in November, the day after Guy Fawkes. Outside the window a spent rocket lay on the lawn. Do you remember how Robert liked to collect empty fireworks and sniff the gunpowder in their cardboard tubes?

A man answered the phone. That gave me a jolt; for some reason I hadn't thought that Stella was married. He didn't seem curious and said that his wife was at work and would be back at three.

By mid-afternoon I was in a dither of nerves and nearly flunked it. As you know, I'm not much of a drinker, but I poured myself a whisky and dialled her number.

I'd prepared a little speech but when I heard Stella's voice I simply blurted out: 'I'm Mrs Wentworth, can we meet?'

There was a long pause. I wondered if her husband was

in the room. She suggested the Wimpy bar next to Cardiff station and we agreed on the next Tuesday lunchtime.

The day arrived and I hadn't felt so nervous since my Finals. Over breakfast you asked me my plans. For the first time, it was ME who lied. I wondered if you, too, had felt the same sense of utter desolation, and yet a tiny, illicit frisson.

I wore that grey dress that you said made me look like a registrar. On the train I thought about my dreams of a career and what I'd given up to look after you and the children. I thought, for the hundredth time, how unsuited I was to be a housewife. And this was how you repaid me! As the train clackety-clacked I repeated this to myself, to keep my anger at boiling point. And-this-is-how-you-repay-me. It was the only way I was going to be able to face that woman.

She was a dumpy little thing, wasn't she? You must have been desperate. That was my first thought when she came through the door. Mousy hair, coat buttoned up tight, nose reddened by the Arctic wind outside. But then she saw me and know what? Her face broke into a smile and she was transformed.

And she rallied. No doubt she realised that this was inappropriate. But I could see that she was normally a friendly sort of person, and even more nervous than me. She perched opposite, handbag on lap, ready to flee at a moment's notice, and asked me politely about my journey.

She kept her eyes on the menu. 'I'm ever so sorry, Mrs Wentworth.'

'So you should be.'

She looked up. 'You're different to what I expected.'

'So he talks about me?'

'No. Not a lot. But I think about you.'

'You do, do you? And my children?'

She nodded.

'Maybe you should have thought about them before you started all this,' said Anna.

'I'm so sorry—'

'Stop saying sorry!'

Stella jumped. The waitress came and they ordered Wimpys, hers with cheese.

It was warm in there and Stella unbuttoned her coat. Anna glimpsed a frilly cream blouse and large breasts. James once called hers Norfolk and Suffolk. It didn't seem cruel; he said it with such love that she'd burst out laughing. They were lying in bed in Green Street, their little room an everywhere, sunshine flooding in and their landlady's vacuum cleaner droning downstairs. *My face in thine eye, thine in mine appears,*' he said, leaning on his elbow and gazing at her, '*And true plain hearts do in the faces rest.*'

'Would you like this?'

Anna jerked to attention. Stella was offering her a handkerchief.

'No thank you.' Anna wiped her eyes and pulled herself together. 'Does your husband know what's been happening?'

'No!' Stella stared at her. 'Don't tell him, it would break his heart.'

'Oh, yes, as opposed to you not breaking mine?'

'I'm sorry—'

'Do shut up! If you were sorry, you'd stop.'

Stella bent down and rummaged in her handbag. Anna gazed at the top of her head. She imagined James's fingers stroking her hair. Stroking the Alps of her breasts.

'Do you smoke?'

Stella was holding out a packet of cigarettes. Players No. 6.

Anna took one. 'I don't in front of James. He disapproves.'

'Yes, same with me.'

'It's a bit rich, considering he puffs away on cigars at college dinners. Talk about double standards.'

Anna stopped. What on earth was she doing, confiding in the woman?

Stella leaned forward, flicked her lighter and lit Anna's cigarette. Anna inhaled and felt her very bones relax.

'You ever smoked Sobranies?' she asked.

'What's Sobranies?'

'Never mind.'

The food arrived. As the waitress put it down they chatted away as if they'd just met up for shopping. Stella told Anna that her husband was a postman but he'd ricked his back, double-digging their allotment. She said that she'd been working in the university canteen. She said she'd liked it there, she liked being surrounded by students.

'They were so young, bless them, and trying to act so grown-up.' She blew out smoke from the corner of her mouth. 'They made me come over all motherly. You see, Ken and I haven't been blessed.'

Had James ever seen his mistress cry? Anna suspected not. With those two, no doubt, it was all fun and frolics.

It was a startling sight. For suddenly the tears erupted and literally spilled down Stella's face, streaking her cheeks with mascara. She said: 'Oh, Mrs Wentworth, I want a baby so much.'

Have one of mine! Anna wanted to shout. Robert and Phoebe had been running her ragged – Robert goading Phoebe, Phoebe bursting into hysterical tears, the usual torment.

'For Ken, too,' Stella said. 'It would make him so happy. He can't have children, you see.' She paused. 'We don't tell people that.'

'Why have you told me, then?'

'I don't know.'

She couldn't offer Stella a handkerchief because she didn't have one. Besides, the woman seemed oblivious, sitting there with her streaming, striped face. Some Teddy boys got up and jostled their way out like a herd of bullocks.

'I'm sorry about that,' Anna said, stubbing out her cigarette. Players No. 6 were disgusting, she'd forgotten that. 'But we have to realise that life's not fair.'

'Maybe your husband will give me one.'

For a moment, Anna thought she had misheard her.

Stella wiped her eyes, leaving smears of mascara on her cheeks. 'I shouldn't be saying this, but it's been at the back of my mind.'

'Does he know this?'

'No. But if something happens, well, I'd be on Cloud Nine.' She ground out her cigarette. 'I told him I'm wearing a coil.'

'Are you?'

She shook her head.

Anna glared at her. 'So *you've* been cheating on *him*.' Ridiculously, she felt a tiny flare of loyalty to James. Only for a second. 'So, what's your husband going to say if you suddenly get pregnant?'

'He's a Christian,' Stella said blandly. 'He'll forgive me.'

'Just because he's a Christian? Haven't you read your history books?'

'You don't know my Ken. He loves me so much he'll forgive me anything. And he'd do anything for a baby, too.'

There was something annoying about her cocky self-assurance. Anna's fleeting sympathy for her vanished.

'So you're using *two* men,' she snapped. 'Congratulations.'

'You don't know what it's like, Mrs Wentworth.' Stella leaned forward, her voice urgent. 'It's like an ache in my belly, all the time. It's like this big hollow inside, it's making me ill and it's getting worse. It's so bad that if I do get pregnant and Ken does kick me out I won't mind because at least I'll have a baby. Do you understand?'

This meeting wasn't going as Anna had expected. But then, what *had* she expected?

'So you're using my husband as a sperm donor,' she said. 'That's why you chose him?'

'No! I fell for him, Mrs Wentworth, hook, line and sinker. He's such a great guy—'

'Yes, I do know that.'

'He makes me feel so clever—'

'He does that with everybody—'

'– it's like, I love my Ken but he's not got a clue what's going on in my head and, to be perfectly frank, I don't think he's that interested. Same with most of them. Then along comes this brilliant man – I knew it the moment I met him. He was in the canteen—'

'Shut up! I don't want to hear the details.' She did, of course, but they would make her throw up.

Stella gazed at her glass of Pepsi. 'I don't know what he saw in me – I'm being quite honest here. I mean, you're such a beautiful lady, much more beautiful than me, and much cleverer. You've got such class, why would he want me?'

'For sex, silly.'

Stella looked up. 'Pardon?'

'To service his carnal needs. Isn't it obvious?'

Stella stared at her.

Anna, too, was taken aback. But something strange was happening in that hot, steamy café in a foreign city. Two cups of coffee had made her light-headed. She wasn't normally reckless, but she was in a heightened state, sitting opposite a woman with whom she had nothing and everything in common. Who she would never see again. Stella had confided in her and now she confided in Stella.

And out it came, in a rush.

'We love each other dearly, James and I,' she said. 'But that side of things has never been the heart of our marriage and it's now more or less over. Not hugs, not closeness, we'll always have those and they mean the world to me. But I've never told him why I've had such difficulty with that – I've never told a living soul – but I'm telling you because you love him and I'm giving you permission to give him what he needs. In fact, it's a huge relief, because you and I are sort of in this together, though I suspect we'll never meet again, after today.'

Stella's mouth hung open. She'd wiped her smeared cheeks but Anna felt a perverse desire to make those tears spill down her face again.

'You see, I was raped when I was eleven,' she said. 'I was raped by a friend of my father's, who took me butterfly-hunting. His name was Dudley. We'd had lunch at his house in Sussex. Afterwards, when the others played tennis, he took me into the woods to look for pearl-bordered fritillaries. He knew I loved butterflies and I'd never seen one. He said they were shy little creatures. "Just like you," he said. I thought that was a bit funny but then grown-ups *were* funny. When we were out of sight of his house he pushed me onto the ground. I thought he'd tripped on a tree root – he was a big man – and tried to help him up. But he pushed me back down. I thought, he's a bit drunk, it's some sort of game. Then I got frightened. He pressed his knuckles against my throat and I suddenly thought he was going to strangle me. Then I thought, of course he won't strangle me, he knows my parents.' Anna paused for breath, her heart hammering. The two Wimpys sat cooling on their plates, their buns starting to wrinkle. 'Then he pulled off my knickers and unzipped his trousers and I saw this *thing*. He wanted me to see it. So purple and angry. It hurt like hell. I was a virgin, of course. And then he pulled me up and patted my bottom and whispered – I remember his boozy breath – he pressed his face against my ear and whispered, "If you tell anybody I'll cut your pretty little eyes out." So I didn't. Until now.'

Stella made a small noise in her throat. She wasn't crying, however. Anna felt released, as if she could float up to the ceiling. She'd offloaded it onto this woman, for reasons she would never understand. To punish her? Shock her? Get her sympathies? Or to ease the guilt for both of them and bind them together in a clammy, sick sort of bond?

'What happened to him?' asked Stella.

'He and his family moved to France and I never saw him again.'

Ah, but it was a relief to speak about it, to say his name. Dudley, Dudley, Dudley. To open herself and spill out her fetid, steaming guts in front of this startled young woman.

Anna pushed back her chair and stumbled to the toilets. Flinging open the door, she dropped to her knees and vomited down the pan. It turned out she was in the Gents; when she emerged, a man stepped out of the next cubicle, zipping up his flies.

She kissed Stella goodbye. Stella looked startled, but rallied and gave her a hug, her breasts pressing against her coat. She was so small; for a mad moment Anna wanted to stroke her hair.

Striding towards the railway station, Anna thought: did I really give her permission to sleep with my husband? In those very words? I went to Cardiff, sabre rattling, and ended up commiserating with this woman about babies and then unloading my deepest and most disgusting violation. What on earth was I doing?

And by urging Stella to keep it a secret – the meeting, the confidences – the two of them had become inappropriately close. She should have simply told the woman to lay off her husband. She should have asked her the obvious question: do you really expect James to leave his family and run off with you?

No, it hadn't gone as planned. But then, what does?
And she kept her secret to the grave.

The letter to James continued:

We ordered something to eat, though I suspect neither of us was hungry. I'd presumed I'd lose my temper and tell her to lay off my husband, but we found ourselves chatting about this and that. She knew I was a keen gardener, you must have told her that, and she wanted my advice about what to plant in a small back yard. North-facing. She said she didn't have a clue but wanted to surprise her husband, of whom she seemed very fond. Then we talked about the scenic delights of the Shrewsbury to Swansea Heritage Railway.

After a while I wondered if your name was ever going to come up, so I asked her what she was planning to do. She jumped like a startled rabbit and started to say how sorry she was and how she didn't want anyone to be hurt, that sort of rubbish. It's then that I surprised her.

You see, I presumed she knew about the state of our marriage. I presumed you'd told her, not least because it excused your seeking solace elsewhere. I imagined it would have made you both feel a whole lot better.

But you were obviously far too British to talk about things like that. Perhaps you were being loyal to me, the frigid wife. Perhaps you thought it reflected badly on yourself, that our lovemaking had pretty well ceased, for all these years.

Perhaps – I've just thought of this – you didn't want her

247

to think it was simply a sex thing, because you weren't 'getting it' at home.

Anyway, she had no idea. Nor do I know if this made her feel better or worse. Not my problem, really.

You won't believe this but we parted on perfectly cordial terms. She even wrote down my suggestion of 'Hydrangea anomala' as a suitable climber for a shady wall.

And she kept her word, I'll give you that. You knew nothing about my little tryst, did you? I would have sensed it if you had. You carried on as usual, disappearing a couple of times a week with your flimsy excuses. But I felt differently now. I'd met her, you see, and lanced the boil. There's nothing as powerful as the imagination and mine had created a collection of demon women. Now they'd evaporated and it was such a relief. Stella was just a normal human being and I could cope with that.

I suspected that your affair would run its course, though it took longer than I expected. I knew when it did because I found you in the spare room sobbing your heart out. You were startled to see me and gabbled something about a colleague of yours having cancer. You used those words, 'a colleague of mine', which sounded pompous, not like you at all, but you'd been caught on the hop.

I'm sure you remember every miserable detail of that day. I have no idea what the final catalyst had been. Maybe Stella issued an ultimatum; maybe you'd had a row. I'd had no communication with her since that meeting in Cardiff. Staying in touch would have been rather creepy, wouldn't it? Besides, we had nothing in common, except you.

So there it is, my darling.

My poor little secret is out, and I know you'll keep it. Why should our dear children and grandchildren be both-ered by what happened so very long ago, in a world before mobile phones and the internet? A quaintly antique world where you could rent a room for £2 a week and get a job at the click of your fingers? The world today is so tough and brutal, compared to ours. That's the received wisdom, anyway. I suspect we were just more adept at covering things up. For we were certainly experts at that.

Did you have another affair? I have no idea, but I saw no signs of it. Our long and engrossing marriage continued for fifty more years, our rollercoaster of love with its highs and its lows, but throughout it we always talked. Always. Except for that one silence.

And, as you know, my difficulties with our children grew easier as time passed. I grew into them, and they into me. We made our peace with each other, if such a peace were necessary. Needless to say, Alice and Jack have brought me nothing but joy. The simplest joy of my life. That's what people say about grandchildren, and they're right. God knows what they'd think, if they read this. The idea of old people's sex lives would turn their stom-achs. To them we're just two harmless old crocks pottering around our Cotswold garden to the strains of Radio 4. And how heavenly that has been.

For it has. Goodbye, darling heart. Forgive me, as I've forgiven you. Thank you. I love you.

Robert

They never knew if their father had opened it. The envelope was stuck down, which implied he hadn't. On the other hand, it was not stuck down that firmly. This could be the result of the glue drying, over the years. Or that he had read it.

Not surprisingly, the two of them preferred the first option. Their mother had put the letter where she'd hoped James would find it. Her death, however, had resulted in the usual tumultuous distractions. Perhaps the letter had fallen behind his desk and the cleaner had shoved it into a drawer. Who knew? Their father was absent-minded at the best of times, and in those raw early days he was barely able to function.

They clung to this scenario. The thought that their father had read it, and misled them yet again, was too horribly painful.

As indeed was their mother's letter. So they had two parents who'd lied to them, and indeed to each other. Their wounds had barely been stitched up before they were opened again. They'd considered their mother a mistress of probity – she was a JP, for Christ's sake! But now this woman who sat in judgement over others was revealed to be as devious as those who sat quivering in front of her.

Robert felt weirdly derailed. Worse than this, it seemed he was a whiney little boy and impossible to love. 'Aren't mothers supposed to love you whatever you're like, isn't that the point of them?' he said. 'She banged on enough about her love for Dad, about their great adventure and long fucking conversation. We talked too!'

They were sitting on the steps of his caravan. 'I suppose we should feel sorry for her,' said Phoebe.

No doubt they would, in time. But just now he and Phoebe weren't in the mood. Pulled back into the past, they felt buffeted and seasick. They sat, slumped against each other. Through the hedge they heard the sound of crashing glass as people threw their bottles into the bins.

The next day, sorting through the paperwork, they found another envelope.

This one had certainly been opened because it had been slit across the top with a paper-knife. It was postmarked Solihull and addressed to their mother.

Inside was a photograph of a newborn baby. On the back was written *Amanda (Mandy) Jane Gatterson b. 12.11.1967.*

Nothing more.

So their mother knew, all the time. And maybe their father did, from the very beginning.

Phoebe had decided to find the whole thing hilarious. This unsettled Robert; now he felt that he didn't know *her* at all. He was feeling increasingly lonely in his little caravan.

'You're being very uptight,' she said. 'Why don't you tell Jack and Alice? I bet they'll find it fascinating.'

'You don't have children, you don't understand. They need to trust their elders.'

She burst out laughing. 'You really are a pompous prick.'

'What, tell them their frigid grandmother pimped her husband's mistress back to him?'

'You really see it like that?'

'And knew about his secret love child?

'*Love child!* What century are you in?'

'And that everybody lied to everybody else? What sort of example does *that* set?'

'You think they need examples? They seem to be doing pretty well on their own.' Her voice rose. 'In fact, *they're* the ones who should be giving *us* an example. They're so non-judgemental, compared to us! And kind and forgiving! And unscrewed up about sex! I mean, half of them seem to be bi and they don't give a toss about that! And changing gender all over the place.'

Now it was Robert who burst out laughing. 'Good God, sis, you *are* firing on all cylinders. What's got into you – got a bloke or something?'

She glared at him. 'Why do men always think that?'

Phoebe

Actually, Robert was right. Phoebe had been seeing a man called Gareth. She'd met him at the recycling centre, out on the bypass; Gareth was newly divorced and unloading his ex-wife's clutter. His children, too, had long since grown up so into the *Landfill Only* skip went broken boxes of broken toys and jigsaws with pieces missing. Gareth said he was downsizing and moving into a flat above the incense shop in the High Street.

They started talking when Phoebe's cardboard box burst open and her father's paperwork spilled out. Gareth helped her gather it up. They were both unburdening themselves of their past. It was a melancholy moment, seeing possessions turned to junk, and she'd been thinking about her father.

She hadn't cried at his funeral. It was time for him to go, that was why. He'd been dreading the indignities of old age, indignities that Mandy had itemised in brutal detail. He'd travelled far enough down that road to know he didn't want to travel further. And he'd felt no pain. So why should one cry for a life so well lived?

That's what she was thinking on that windy October day, the obligatory *Guardian*s swirling around the *Paper and Cardboard Only* container and the lorries thundering past.

Gareth wasn't really her type. A retired solicitor, no less, in one of those quilted jackets that retired solicitors wear. But they started talking, wandered down to The Coffee Cup and carried on talking for the rest of the morning. Then they crossed the High Street to Angie's Bistro, had some lunch and talked some more. It certainly made a change from Torren, from whom she'd parted as unknown as when she'd arrived.

The next day Gareth showed her his flat, three empty rooms smelling of new carpet, a stage set for the next period of his life. Opposite was the butcher's shop, behind which she lived. It was laughably convenient.

A few weeks later she told Robert she was having a thing with a solicitor and would he like his dog? She was a spaniel called Connie. Under the terms of the lease she wasn't allowed in the flat and Gareth's ex didn't want her.

'She's not the obligatory lurcher but she's highly intelligent and you said you'd love a dog again.'

But Robert wasn't listening. 'A thing? Blimey, who is he? Where did you meet him?'

Strictly speaking it wasn't 'a thing' but she didn't tell Robert this. When Gareth stayed over, the two of them lay chastely in each other's arms. It reminded her of the boy she spent all night kissing in that tent a thousand years ago. Her life seemed to have come full circle. In those days, however, it was frustrated passion; now it was passion spent. For it was simply human warmth that the two of them seem to crave. They had both been hurt; they seemed to have slipped straight into companionship. And what a miracle, simply to be friends with a man! Something that had eluded her all her life, and what was wrong with that? After all, her parents remained devoted throughout their *mariage blanc.*

Instead, they spent half the night talking. Insomnia was another thing that worsened with age, another thing nobody mentioned. She thought: the world is full of old people lying in the dark, waiting for the first birds to sing.

Robert

How great that Phoebe was having sex again! Cheeks flushed, eyes bright, she was throbbing with pheromones and looked ten years younger. It was hard to believe, but that portly little solicitor must be dynamite in the sack. Bully for him, Robert thought.

His sister was changing in other ways too. Happier and less tense, which was to be expected. But in her case, sexual gratification seemed to be leading to a social conscience. This was not a common trajectory, but then Phoebe was an unusual woman. What had happened, however, surprised even him.

For she seemed to be giving up the painting and devoting herself to public life. 'Who needs another watercolour of bloody sheep,' she said, 'when the Scout Hut's falling down?'

He could understand this because Knockton had a great community spirit. Coming from London, this had been a revelation. Everybody knew everybody, they were always bustling around delivering casseroles to the bereaved and fixing each other's cars. Only the day before, he went into the gift shop to buy Buffy a birthday card and Gilly, the owner, said: 'Somebody's got him the Van Gogh already, you'd better choose another one.' No doubt some people would find this claustrophobic but it made a change from his street in Wimbledon where *community* meant gated.

And now, blow me down, the woman wanted to become a Town Councillor! Phoebe, his sister! He presumed it was the influence of this Gareth chap but she snapped back: 'Do you really think I'm defined by men?'

She said the seeds were sown during the supermarket protest and grew from there. She said the world was full of second-rate artists and that Mandy had given her a reality check.

'Reality check? Mandy?'

'She made me realise that I was just dicking about and I wasn't really happy. She was doing something so worthwhile – caring for Dad, organising things in his village, being kind and useful. She said that happiness was like coke, it was a by-product of something else.'

'Aldous Huxley said that, not her.'

'But that's how she lived her life, and we sneered at her because she watched daytime TV and went to Nando's. You and me, we're such snobs.'

'You're getting very Ken Loach. The working class isn't necessarily noble; don't fall for that one.'

'Don't be such a cynic.'

This spiralled off into a row, which then subsided as they drained the bottle and departed on cordial terms. They were brother and sister; they were used to this.

But to Robert's astonishment – and hers – Phoebe got elected. This was apparently due to the poisonous nature of local politics. Knockton looked such a friendly place but lift the lid and in fact it was a nest of vipers. That's what he was told by Caradoc, an amiable old alcoholic with whom he watched the footie in the pub. Caradoc used to be a reporter on the local paper and knew a thing or two. 'Don't be fooled,' he said. 'They'd slit each other's throats if they got a chance.' He said there were feuds going back years, old farming families stealing land from each other, poaching sheep and poaching wives, poisoning wells and snitching on each other to the authorities. Robert wished they'd met before he'd started on his ill-fated novel. Caradoc's words had the stench of truth, something that had evaded him for four long years as he toiled in his shed.

Phoebe, however, was an outsider and thus uncontaminated. So her sketches were swept aside and replaced with files from Powys County Council. Robert was impressed. She even drove to Debenhams in Hereford and bought herself a suit. A *suit*.

Robert shared this news with Connie, *his* new love. God, it was good to have a dog again. Spaniels were highly intelligent; Connie listened to him, head tilted, eyes bright, silky ears so seductive to his touch. She had instantly forgotten her previous master; she was now devoted to Robert and had become his one and only fan. When he sat at his laptop she pushed her head under the table and laid her chin on his knee, gazing at him as if he were Saul Bellow. It beat women any day.

Phoebe

Another weird thing was happening. Phoebe and her brother seemed to be swapping places. She now had a navy-blue suit and a solicitor boyfriend; it was Robert who was turning into an old hippie. Better late than never, she thought.

He was certainly making up for lost time. His hair was longer and he'd grown a beard. He'd got a dog. He was still in his caravan; he'd given their father's inheritance to his children, so they could survive in London. When he was not writing his novel – which might be unreadable, for all she knew – he sat on the step whittling wood. He was the happiest she'd ever known him.

This might have been due to the pulling power of a man in a caravan, for her brother had become something of a pussy-magnet – his term, needless to say. What was it about confined spaces? No possessions, no memories, just the *now*. Huts, caravans, that tent where long ago she had one of the most intense experiences of her life. *My little tent an every where.*

Robert seemed to be just as surprised as she was by the number of women making their way across his orchard. Only yesterday she'd seen a familiar car parked by the gate. It belonged to Pam, the quilt-maker.

CAVAN COUNTY LIBRARY

But at my back I always hear
Times wingèd chariot hurrying near;
And yonder all before us lie
Deserts of vast eternity.

Her father in the garden, reading aloud. Her mother, straightening up from her weeding and pushing the hair out of her face. That rare, dazzling smile. Just for him.